"Somehow, I p
differently."

She shrugged, maintaining her pretense of nonchalance when what she really wanted was to find a quiet, dark closet to hide in until her insides quit trembling. She could just imagine her reaction had it been a real engagement.

Devin stared into her face, his brows knitting as they did when he was working out a problem in his head.

"What? Having second thoughts?" Her heart stuttered to a stop and she held her breath. Not like the engagement was real or anything. "That's bad when you're having second thoughts about an engagement that really isn't. Does the thought of a Kendall marrying a lowly executive assistant go against the grain?" She tried to laugh, failing miserably.

He shook his head. "No. I was thinking we should seal this deal in some way." His frown lifted and he leaned closer, his hand rising to cup the back of her neck, drawing her closer. "Perhaps with a kiss."

ELLE JAMES

ENGAGED WITH THE BOSS

TORONTO NEW YORK LONDON
AMSTERDAM PARIS SYDNEY HAMBURG
STOCKHOLM ATHENS TOKYO MILAN MADRID
PRAGUE WARSAW BUDAPEST AUCKLAND

This book is dedicated to the Harlequin Intrigue editors—Denise Zaza
and Allison Lyons—who have shown continued faith and confidence
in my storytelling abilities.
Thank you for your support and encouragement.

Special thanks and acknowledgment to Elle James for her contribution
to the Situation: Christmas series.

ISBN-13: 978-0-373-69573-7

ENGAGED WITH THE BOSS

Copyright © 2011 by Harlequin Books S.A.

Recycling programs
for this product may
not exist in your area.

www.Harlequin.com

Printed in U.S.A.

ABOUT THE AUTHOR

A Golden Heart winner for Best Paranormal Romance in 2004, Elle James started writing when her sister issued a Y2K challenge to write a romance novel. She managed a full-time job, raised three wonderful children and she and her husband even tried their hands at ranching exotic birds (ostriches, emus and rheas) in the Texas Hill Country. Ask her, and she'll tell you what it's like to go toe-to-toe with an angry 350-pound bird! After leaving her successful career in information technology management, Elle is now pursuing her writing full-time. She loves building exciting stories about heroes, heroines, romance and passion. Elle loves to hear from fans. You can contact her at ellejames@earthlink.net or visit her website at www.ellejames.com.

Books by Elle James

HARLEQUIN INTRIGUE

CAST OF CHARACTERS

Devin Kendall—CEO of Kendall Communications, and oldest of the Kendall siblings. The anchor in the Kendall family, he's determined to keep his siblings happy and safe from harm, to the detriment of his own happiness.

Jolie Carson—Devin Kendall's talented and competent executive assistant, who has been secretly in love with her boss since the day she started working for him six years ago.

Craig Kendall—Inherited ownership of Kendall Communications upon the death of his brother Joseph Kendall, who was murdered, along with his wife, twenty years ago on Christmas Eve.

Angela Kendall—Craig Kendall's wife, who lost her only child in a car accident twenty years earlier. She took all four Kendall children in and raised them as her own after their parents were murdered.

Ash Kendall—Devin Kendall's brother and a St. Louis Metropolitan Police detective.

Natalie Kendall—Youngest of the Kendall children, she's all grown up and fiercely independent, despite her brothers' attempts to protect her.

Jesse Allen—District attorney bent on finding the murderer responsible for killing Joseph and Marie Kendall twenty years ago.

Letty Morgan—Recently left Kendall Communications after getting caught using drugs by a drug-screening test.

TJ Bryant—Letty Morgan's boyfriend, who has an ax to grind with the Kendalls over the firing of Letty.

Chapter One

Devin Kendall left his office at Kendall Communications late as usual, long after rush hour. When he stepped out into the parking garage, he waved as his uncle Craig drove past.

Weary beyond sanity, Devin climbed into his Lexus SUV and relaxed into the leather bucket seats. As tired as he was, he could fall asleep here. All he had to do was recline the seat and close his eyes.

The temptation was great, considering he hadn't slept much the past few nights. Not with the weight of the world on his shoulders. Or at least the weight of his family's safety, which in Devin's mind was his world.

All these years they'd been so certain the killer who'd taken his parents' lives was off the street, no longer a threat.

That belief had been shattered just a few weeks ago. DNA evidence had proved that Rick Campbell, the man who'd spent the better part of twenty years in jail for the crime, wasn't the one who'd committed the murders. The police had arrested and the jury had sentenced the wrong man. His parents' killer still remained at large.

Devin hadn't slept well since, knowing the killer had been free all this time.

He buckled up, cranked the engine and drove out of the

parking garage onto the streets of downtown St. Louis. He noticed his uncle's car turned left out of the parking garage onto Market Street. As Devin headed east, a car that had been illegally parked on the normally busy street slipped in behind his uncle's four-door BMW sedan.

This late in the evening, it was not unusual for there to be cars moving up and down Market Street. But something about the way the vehicle had slipped in behind his uncle's car had the hairs on the back of Devin's neck standing on end.

The car's driver hadn't switched his lights on. The streetlamps gave out enough light that a person could forget to turn on their headlights, but the feeling scratching across his subconscious wouldn't let Devin rest.

Instead of turning right toward the warehouse district where he lived, Devin made the decision to follow his uncle for a couple blocks. Just in case.

He stayed far enough behind the two cars as not to generate suspicion, until he noticed the vehicle following his uncle didn't have a license plate. Alarm bells sounded in Devin's head. He increased his speed, closing the distance between his SUV and the two cars ahead until he was only a hundred yards behind. He wasn't fast enough.

When his uncle turned north on Jefferson Avenue, the nondescript car behind him sped up. As they rounded the corner, the trailing car rammed into Craig's sedan, slamming the BMW into the traffic light pole. The unlicensed car sped away, leaving a trail of burned rubber.

Devin skidded his Lexus to a halt behind his uncle's vehicle, hit the hazard light switch and jumped out.

"Uncle Craig!" He reached the driver's door as his uncle pounded against it.

Jammed by the impact, the door wouldn't open until Devin braced his foot against the side of the car and yanked with all his might. The door swung open and his uncle looked out at him, the powder of the deployed air bags dusting his hair and face.

"What happened?" Craig asked, fumbling to unclip his seat belt.

Devin leaned in and released the buckle. "That fool just ran you off the road. Are you all right?"

"I'm fine. Just a little shaken." His uncle tried to get out of the car, his face pale, his eyes glazed.

Devin placed a hand on his uncle's shoulder, insisting he remain seated. "I'm calling an ambulance."

"Really, I'm fine. I'd rather go on home to bed. It was just a little accident."

"No way. We need to stay right here while I also call the police. I had a feeling something like this would happen."

"What do you mean?"

"That was no accident. Whoever hit you knew exactly what he was doing. That was a deliberate attack."

"WHAT HAPPENED TO UNCLE Craig last night was no accident." Devin Kendall paced the length of his spacious office. "I don't know about the rest of you, but I haven't slept in days."

"What can we do that isn't already being done?" Craig responded from where he sat on the leather couch, pressing his fingers to his forehead gingerly, lucky he only had a bump on his forehead to show for his collision with the light pole. "The car that hit me hasn't been found—it was too dark to identify the make and model. Basically, the police have nothing to go on."

Devin's family had gathered for this meeting at his request. The twentieth anniversary of his parents' murders loomed like a ghostly specter with teeth that could come back to bite any one of the Kendalls—and apparently had in the attack on his uncle the previous night.

Devin stopped pacing and faced his family. "The person who killed our parents is still out there. And things are becoming much more dangerous since Rick Campbell's murder."

Though he had been exonerated of the crime for which he'd served almost twenty years, Campbell had not been able to revel in his release as he himself was killed just days afterward.

Devin's sister, Natalie, leaned forward in the wing-backed chair beside the couch. "Whoever did it hasn't made a move on the rest of us." With her long straight blond hair and green eyes, Natalie was the spitting image of their dead mother. And, she could more than hold her own in a marketing meeting with the executives of the multimillion-dollar corporation, Kendall Communications.

But Devin wasn't so sure she could stand up against a cold-blooded murderer. "What if the killer decides the police are getting too close? What if one of us reminds him too much of our parents and he decides to kill again?"

"You're borrowing trouble, Dev." His brother Ash shook his head. "The St. Louis Metropolitan Police have reopened the case. We're working it."

Devin snorted. "No offense, Ash, but they arrested the wrong man twenty years ago. What makes you think they can figure it out now?"

Ash's lips thinned into a straight line and his eyes narrowed at Devin. "This time, we don't have a celebrity-seeking cop investigating. And we're not kids ready to accept any answer."

His chest tightened as Devin recalled the morning he'd learned his parents had been murdered. Guilt wadded like a fist in his throat and he had to swallow several times to clear it in order to speak.

He'd been out all night and sneaked back into the house only to find their bodies. Natalie had been standing in mute shock. If only he'd been there, he might have been able to stop the murderer and spared his little sister the horror.

Devin wished his brother Thad was there. As usual, Thad was off on a journalism assignment with no expected return date and limited ability to contact.

Jolie Carson, Devin's executive assistant, appeared at his side with a cup of coffee. Just her presence helped to ease his discomfort. She'd been his best hire to date. Six years and counting, she'd stood by him, organized his schedule and his life to the point he couldn't imagine functioning without her. He took the coffee mug from her. "Thanks."

Devin took a sip of the coffee. Black, with a hint of cinnamon, just the way he liked it. "We aren't kids anymore." He set the mug on the desk and crossed his arms over his chest. "But that might make us more of a target."

"What do you suggest we do?" Natalie's eyebrows rose up her forehead. "Hide in our homes until the real killer is brought to justice?" She stood, her shoulders back, twin flags of color in her cheeks. "I'm not going to run scared just because some lunatic is out there. Twenty years is a long time. If he was going to make a move on any of the rest of us, he'd have done it by now. I have a job, as do the rest of you."

Jolie stopped on her way out of the office. "She's right. You can't run scared or the killer wins."

Devin scowled at Jolie. She propped a hand on her hip, her lips firm, her chin held high, daring him to contradict her in front of his family.

He'd have a talk with Jolie when everyone cleared out of his office. Her advice was usually sound and he valued her opinion, but she didn't understand how dangerous the situation could get.

"Natalie and Jolie are right." Craig stood, as well. "Much as I hate that we haven't found the killer, we can't live in fear. We have lives. We have a business to run."

If Devin could, he'd lock his family up on the Kendall estate until the killer was found. He leaned toward telling them just that, but knew they'd fight him tooth and nail. The Kendall stubborn streak was strong in every one of them. It's what made them successful. They didn't give up and they didn't run scared. Unfortunately, that didn't make him worry any less.

The tension in his shoulders loosened and he sighed. "Just do me a favor, will you?"

His siblings and uncle waited before committing to the favor.

"Be careful. Watch your backs and don't take anything for granted. If you see anything or anyone suspicious, let me or Ash know immediately. You can't be too cautious." His message was for all of them, but his gaze landed on Natalie.

She frowned. "I'm always careful. Just try to attack me and let's see who ends up on his butt." She waved him forward, her stance hampered by her slim-fitting skirt.

Jolie chuckled. "I'm scared."

"Me, too." Ash clapped his sister on her back. "Natalie is a black belt."

"Training and defending are completely different." Devin's gaze darkened. Natalie was his little sister. He still felt responsible for her safety even though she was a fully grown twenty-six-year-old.

"I think he's chicken," Natalie confided to Ash, her

gaze on Devin, a smile lurking at the corners of her mouth. "But I'll let it slide this time. I'd hate to damage my favorite skirt." She cocked her head at him. "Anything else, dear brother?"

"Yeah, I need that marketing plan by end of day. I suggest you get to work before the CEO fires you."

She laughed. "Anyone ever tell the CEO he's a pain in the butt?"

"That could be construed as insubordination." Devin shot a wad of paper at her. "Get out of here."

Natalie spun on her sensible heel and headed for the door, stopping long enough to ask Jolie, "We still on for dinner tonight?"

"You bet. I've been dying to try that new Hunan restaurant around the corner."

"Me, too." Natalie turned back toward her brothers. "And, don't worry, I'll have eyes in the back of my head."

Craig buttoned his suit jacket. "I'm sorry this has all come up again. Your aunt Angela is beside herself with worry."

"Like Natalie said, we can take care of ourselves." Ash draped an arm over his uncle's shoulder. "You and Aunt Angela have done so much for this family. I'm more worried about you than the rest of us."

Craig and Angela had taken on the responsibility of raising the Kendall children upon the death of their parents.

"I beefed up the security at the estate," Craig said. "I'm considering hiring a bodyguard, but Angela is dead set against it."

Natalie paused in the doorway. "Can't blame her." She shuddered. "I'd hate having someone following me around, anticipating my every move. It would drive me nuts." She glanced at Jolie. "Six o'clock, then. Bye."

Jolie smiled and closed the door behind Natalie. She had her wavy red hair pulled back in a neat bun, exposing the long length and porcelain skin of her neck.

For a moment, Devin studied the way an errant curl bounced against her earlobe and wondered what she looked like with her hair down. She was somewhat plain in her soft gray suit with a proper slim-line skirt cut to the knee. Everything about Jolie was proper except her wicked sense of humor and her ability to tell him like it was. She didn't pull her punches.

He liked that about her. Jolie Carson didn't take any guff from him or anyone else.

"I'm out of here. Duty calls." Ash, always assuming his role as the cop, headed for the door. "I'm still digging through the case file hoping I find something they missed. I'll start interviewing witnesses again soon."

"Can you keep us up-to-date on how it goes?" Devin asked.

"You bet." Ash crossed the room and just as he reached for the door handle, Natalie crashed back in.

"You aren't going to believe this." She walked to the large television screen mounted on the wall, flicked it on and fumbled with the remote until she had a picture of the local district attorney at what appeared to be a press conference in front of the St. Louis courthouse.

A reporter pushed a mike in his face. "We understand the Christmas Eve Murders case has been reopened. What are you and the St. Louis Metropolitan Police Department doing to solve this case?"

The D.A. stood straight and looked directly into the camera. "As you all have heard, with the latest forensic evidence, the state crime lab was able to rule out Rick Campbell as the murderer. The St. Louis Metropolitan

Police Department has reopened and is actively investigating the case again. We'll get our murderer."

"Any guesses as to who might have done it?" another reporter asked.

"It's too early to say at this time. Let the detectives do their work." The D.A.'s eyebrows lowered, his eyes darkening. "But we'll look at everyone involved with the Kendall family. As in the majority of murder cases, many times it's someone close to the family, usually a family member who commits the crime."

Natalie and Jolie gasped.

Devin, Ash and Craig all swore.

"That SOB. How dare he cast suspicion on the Kendalls." Natalie's cheeks flamed and her hands fisted. "I'd like to have a word with that man."

Jolie shook her head. "Perhaps he's after the publicity. Bashing the Kendalls is a sure way to get the cameras turned your way."

"But why?" Natalie stared at the man on the screen. "He's not up for reelection this year."

"No, and he wouldn't get my vote even if he was." Devin flicked the television off. "Don't let it worry you. They don't have anything on any one of us."

"Yeah, but the media will be following us, just in case they find some dirt somewhere," Uncle Craig said. "If they don't find dirt, they might just make something up to sensationalize a slow-news night."

"Be extra vigilant with your safety and keep your nose clean." Devin shot a stern look at his siblings. "Don't get caught in a situation where you're cornered by the paparazzi."

Ash snorted. "Easier said than done. Later, brother." He grabbed Devin's hand and shook it, then pulled him close. "Get some rest. You look like hell."

"Thanks, you don't look so good yourself. Keep an eye on that fiancée of yours. She could be in as much danger as the rest of us. Especially since she found the DNA evidence that freed Rick Campbell."

"Rachel can hold her own. But I'll gladly keep a very close eye on her." Ash waggled his eyebrows.

Devin shook his head. "How she puts up with you, I'll never know."

Ash smiled at Jolie. "My big brother hasn't learned that a good woman makes a man want to be a better person. That woman could be right under his nose and he hasn't pulled his head out of the sand long enough to notice." He winked at Devin. "Am I right?"

"Shut up and get out." Devin shook his head, a hint of a smile pulling at his lips. Ash was a ladies' man who'd met his match in Rachel. That didn't mean Devin was headed down the matrimonial path. He had too much on his plate to even think of a relationship.

His gaze landed on Jolie. She was the ideal woman, the one he found himself measuring all others by. *If* he decided to settle down and think about a wife and two-point-one children, he'd like to find someone as strong and stable as Jolie. But that was a big *if,* one he didn't intend to explore anytime in the near future.

And she was his executive assistant. Completely off-limits in the corporate world. He shuddered inwardly at the media nightmare such a relationship would generate.

JOLIE SAT ACROSS THE restaurant table from Natalie, laughing and chatting. Yet her thoughts were of Devin, whom she'd left in his office thirty minutes earlier. She really should have stayed to see if he needed anything.

"He'll be fine. You know, you aren't married to him or

the job." Natalie smiled at Jolie's attempt to eat Chinese the traditional way.

"I understand why the Chinese are so thin," Jolie grumbled, fumbling with the chopsticks. She almost managed to get four grains of rice to her lips before the chopsticks slipped and the rice fell into her lap. What was the use? "I give up. I'm hopeless at this. I can't even pretend to be sophisticated and a world traveler."

"Not to worry. That's what they make forks for." Natalie handed her the fork beside her plate.

Jolie held her hand up. "No. I'm going to eat with the chopsticks or go hungry." She put the sticks together and used them as a shovel, this time getting a line of rice and vegetables into her mouth without too much spillage.

"So what did you think about my brother's family meeting?"

Jolie shrugged. "I don't know what to think about the whole situation."

"Oh, come on. Are you telling me Jolie Carson doesn't have an opinion? That's a change."

Jolie grinned. "Okay, I do, but I didn't want to speak out against Devin. He's been taking this all to heart. The man hasn't slept in days. Probably hasn't eaten."

"Oh, so the dinner-to-go you ordered isn't for your freezer then, is it?" Natalie smiled. "Don't worry. I won't hold that little lie against you. You're going by my brother's condo to make sure he gets a proper meal."

Jolie's cheeks burned.

Natalie leaned across the table and grabbed Jolie's hand. "Have you told him how you feel about him?"

"I don't know what you mean." Jolie pulled her hand from her friend's.

"Sorry, I'm not buying it." Natalie stared hard into Jolie's face. "You're in love with him, aren't you?"

Jolie considered lying again but thought better of it. Her friend deserved the truth, no matter how pathetic it was. She sighed. "For six years."

"Good grief. When are you going to tell him?"

"Never." Jolie sat up straight and pointed a finger at Natalie. "And neither are you."

"Not tell him? What good will that do?"

"I work for the man. If he thinks I'm in love with him, he'll fire me on the spot."

"And you'd rather work as his executive assistant, secretly in love with him, than work somewhere else. Right?"

Jolie's lips twisted. "Pathetic, huh?"

Natalie leaned her chin on her palm and sighed. "No, I think it's romantic. I wish I could find someone I'm completely crazy about."

"You will. He'll show up when you're least expecting it."

Natalie sighed again. "I hope it's before I'm as old as you are."

Jolie tossed her napkin at her. "Thanks. I'm feeling older by the second with you around."

"Speaking of showing up—" Natalie sat up straighter, her brow furrowing "—there he is again."

"There's who?" Jolie twisted in her seat.

"That guy at the table by the door."

"The one with the menu over his face." Jolie rolled her eyes.

"Yeah, only he hasn't always had the menu over his face." She lobbed Jolie's napkin back at her. "I swear he's the same guy who's been following me for the past few days."

Jolie looked closer, but the menu remained up, the man studying it intently. A flicker of concern threatened her usual calm. "Have you said anything to your brother?" Devin would want to know if there was any threat to his family.

"No. If I tell him I think I'm being followed, he'll insist on a police escort everywhere I go." Natalie shrugged. "I'll handle it myself rather than be put under lock and key by my overbearing brother."

"He's worried about you." Jolie shot another glance behind her at the menu-covered stranger. "He worries about his family."

"He's annoying and overprotective. You'd think he was my father, not my brother."

"As the oldest, he feels responsible for his siblings."

"Well, he needs to stop it." Natalie set her fork aside. "I have work to do at home. Are you sure you don't mind taking the marketing plan to my brother? I promised I'd have it by the end of the day." She laughed. "Guess late at night is still part of today."

"I'll get it to him." Jolie patted her oversize purse with the file folder inside.

"Yeah, and make sure he eats that food you bring him. He looks like he's losing weight."

"Now who's the worried sibling?" Jolie laughed. "I'll stand over him until he downs every bite."

Natalie grinned. "I can see you doing just that. Like a drill sergeant ready to pounce on him if he doesn't." Then her smile faded. "I have half a mind to tell him to wake up and smell the rose he has for an E.A."

"Don't you dare."

"It goes both ways. Don't tell him I have someone following me unless you want me to tell him that you have a thing for him."

Jolie already regretted telling Natalie about her secret infatuation for her boss. No matter how good it felt to let it out and confess, she saw it for what it was, a wretched situation of unrequited love.

Everyone, especially her, knew that Devin Kendall was married to his job. What time he didn't give to the business, he dedicated to the protection of his family. He didn't have time for himself, much less a relationship. Jolie had known this for a long time and had come to accept it. But having turned thirty on her last birthday, she had heard the beginning ticks of her biological clock. Deep in her heart, she'd always wanted a family…children…a husband who loved her.

She wouldn't get those things from Devin Kendall. He was in a league way above Jolie's humble beginnings. If she was honest with herself, she'd accept that and move on.

She gathered her purse, the to-go bag of his favorite Kung Pao Chicken, and bade Natalie goodbye at her car.

The man who'd been at the table with the menu over his face had left before they did so she didn't get a good look at him. But that didn't make her feel any better about sending Natalie off on her own.

Despite her promise not to tell Devin, she knew she would. Natalie's safety was more important than Jolie's love life.

Or lack thereof.

She dropped her purse and the bag of food on the empty passenger seat, revved the engine of her four-door sedan and then drove toward Devin's condo, trying to squelch the sudden rush of adrenaline and excitement at seeing her boss outside the office environment.

Chapter Two

Devin jumped to his feet when the doorbell rang, grumbling all the way to the entrance, regretting his decision not to buy a condo with a security guard at the front desk. "Who the hell comes by this late at night?"

He yanked the door open, ready to rip into the salesman on the other side and brought himself up short.

Jolie smiled and held up a bag that smelled of soy sauce and spices. "Hungry?"

"What the hell are you doing here so late? I would think that at least one of us would have a life."

She snorted and followed him into the living room. "Like I could have a life. With you calling or texting me every hour of the day and night. Any man I've ever tried to date never understood."

Devin frowned. "You date?"

She thunked the bag of food on the counter in his kitchen and shot a twisted grin his way. "I would if I had a day off."

"What are you doing here?" And why did she look so damned good? Something was different about Jolie, but Devin was too wound up to put his finger on it.

"I brought Natalie's marketing plan by. You wanted it by end of day. It's end of day, in case you hadn't noticed, and here it is." She pulled the document from her voluminous purse and laid it next to the bag of Chinese food containers.

Devin's frown deepened. "Why didn't she bring it herself?"

"She had other plans and your condo is on my way home."

"That's right, you had dinner together."

"We did."

Devin crossed his arms over his chest. The thought of his sister going home alone bothered him. "I don't like it that she's out and about after dark."

"She's twenty-six. Old enough to know how to take care of herself."

"She's my kid sister."

"The key word is *sister.*" Jolie scooped food from the containers onto a clean plate. "You aren't her parent and she's a big girl, not a kid. Give her a break."

"I can't. This whole murder investigation is eating me alive."

"Then get a bodyguard for her and quit worrying." Jolie stared across at him. "She's had a man following her the past few days. It wouldn't hurt to have someone to watch her back. Now, here." She handed him a plate of Kung Pao Chicken and steered him toward the couch. "Sit. Eat. If you still feel like it when your stomach is full, then you can resume your worrying."

He let her push him toward the living room, her fingers warm on his back. He liked the touch a little too much and growled menacingly, feeling as though his attraction to her was a sign of his exhaustion. He'd be better off escorting her to the door as soon as possible before things got complicated. "I don't need you telling me what to do. Just so you know, I'd already decided on a bodyguard."

Jolie grounded her hands on her hips, her stance wide,

fearlessly ready to take him on. "When was the last time you ate?" she demanded.

"Lunch."

She snorted. "You skipped lunch to meet with the board of directors."

He didn't like it when she was right, but the color in her cheeks had heightened, a sure sign she was riled. He did like it when Jolie got riled. The unflappable executive assistant was entirely too tightly bound.

What were they arguing about? Oh, yeah. "We had lunch at the meeting."

"You spoke all the way through the meeting. Bottled water doesn't count." With her shoulders flung back, her head held high and the cut of her blouse dipping low over her breasts, she looked more lively than he could remember. And there was something vastly different about her tonight.

Suddenly feeling the need to rub his executive assistant the wrong way, Devin set the plate in front of him. "I'll eat when I'm hungry."

"When will that be?" She perched on the edge of the coffee table, lifted a forkful of food and held it out. "I'm under orders to stay until you've eaten. So do me a favor and eat this so I can go home."

He opened his mouth to argue and she shoved the fork in.

His eyes widened and then narrowed. He chewed thoughtfully, emitting a soft moan. "Mmm. This is good."

That she was perched on his coffee table, leaning forward in a soft ribbed-knit shirt that showed the rounded curve of her breasts didn't make it easy to swallow. Somehow he managed.

He frowned. "You look different."

"I'm the same old Jolie who's been working with you

for the past six years. How different could I look?" She leveled another forkful of food and raised her eyebrows. "Are you going to feed yourself or am I going to have to?"

He opened his mouth and let her place the fork between his teeth. She always got his blood flowing and made him feel alive, even when he was half-dead with worry and lack of sleep. "How do you do that?"

"Feed you?" She scooped up another forkful of food. "It's easy, just like feeding a baby."

He grabbed her hand, spilling rice onto his lap.

Her eyes widened, her green irises flashing a startling contrast to her pale skin.

"No. I can feed myself." He pulled her closer until her bottom came up off the table and she teetered forward. "How do you go from being my plain executive assistant to this?" He touched her hair, the soft waves curling around his finger. "Ah. It's the hair."

She stared into his eyes, her bottom lip caught between her teeth, her breasts inching dangerously closer to his hand with each breath she took.

If Devin was a gambling man, he'd bet she was as attracted to him as he was to her at that moment.

Holy crap, why hadn't he seen this before? Why had it taken him so long to really look at her?

Jolie Carson had worked for him for six years and this was the first time he'd seen her with her hair down around her shoulders. It totally changed her appearance from the cool, efficient executive assistant, moving determinedly in the background of his life. She'd morphed from the one-person dynamo he relied on so much at work to a softer, more personable and more…hmm…vulnerable woman he'd swear he'd never met.

And yet he had.

She tugged against the hand holding her wrist, her gaze

dropping to his lap. "I'm sorry. I seem to have spilled rice on you." Her hand reached for the food, brushing against his crotch.

The nearness to his arousal made him suck in a breath, his body on alert, his member jerking to attention.

Jolie wrenched her hand back, her pale cheeks flaming. "I didn't mean to touch you there…I mean, I'm sorry… well, hell. If I could be more of a clown, I'd be in a circus." She laughed and backed away so quickly her legs bumped against the coffee table, throwing her off balance.

Devin caught a flailing arm and yanked her forward, her teetering momentum sending her falling toward him, landing hard on his lap.

She scrambled to get up, but Devin's arm hooked around her waist, holding her still. "Relax. I won't bite… unless you want me to." He chuckled, his chest rubbing against her back. A citrusy scent wrapped around his senses. "You smell good." He leaned into her, his nose tickled by the soft red curls. "Why is that?"

"It's my shampoo." She wiggled against him, her bottom grinding into his rising arousal. "I'm fine, really. You can let me up." She sat in his lap, her body rigid, her brows knitted. "Mr. Kendall. I believe you've gone from exhausted to delirious. Let me up."

"So it's Mr. Kendall now, is it?" He knew he should let her go, but her body was so soft against his, all the curves, the scent. The way she moved made him relaxed and excited all at once. Most importantly, it made him forget his troubles if for only a moment.

He could imagine how it would feel to have her long, naked legs wrapped around his middle as he drove into her. Heat filled his groin, pooling low and strong. He wanted her in a way that had nothing to do with PDAs or memos. The CEO in him shut down; the man roared to life.

"Why did you come over tonight?" He leaned into her neck, the temptation to taste more than he could resist. He nibbled the tender skin just below her earlobe.

Her back arched against him, her head dropping back until it rested against his shoulder. "I thought you might be hungry."

"I'm hungry, all right." He nibbled again, nipping at the pulse pounding away at the base of her throat. "But not for food."

He turned her in his arms and cupped her cheeks with his palms. "Where have you been hiding?"

She stared into his eyes, her green ones darkening. "I've been here all along." Her gaze dropped to his lips and her tongue darted out, sliding across her own lips.

Mesmerized by that little pink tongue, Devin couldn't deny tasting it for himself. He pulled her close, capturing her mouth beneath his, his tongue sweeping over the line of her lips until they opened.

He thrust in, conquering her mouth, slanting and sliding in and out, his movements feverish, agitated as if he couldn't get close enough. The barrier of their clothing frustrated him.

His hands found the hem of her shirt and pulled it up and over her head, tossing it to a far corner.

The lacy white bra beneath held her firm breasts high, the rounded swells enticing him past redemption. He twisted, laying her out on the couch beneath him, his mouth traveling the length of her throat, down over her collarbone to the lovely breasts, rising and falling rapidly to the rhythm of her ragged breathing.

"Devin," she gasped as his mouth closed over a nipple

trapped beneath the lace of her bra. "Do you know what you're doing?"

"I would think it obvious."

"You aren't delirious from lack of sleep?" she asked.

"I'm deliriously drunk from you."

"Are you sure this is what you want to do?"

"Never more certain." He reached behind her, flicked the catch to her bra and slid the straps down over her shoulders, her breasts spilling free into his hands. They were pale like porcelain, tipped with strawberry-colored nipples, puckered into tight nubs, ready for plucking.

His mouth descended on one lush, ripe tip, drawing it between his teeth where he rolled it gently, nipping and licking.

A moan rose in her throat and her back arched off the couch, pressing her breast more firmly into his mouth.

All the tension, the worry, the latent frustration bubbled up inside him, driving a sense of urgency to get naked with Jolie, to take her, to ram into her over and over again until his lust was slaked, his desires sated and his energy consumed.

Pale, slim fingers reached out to flick open the buttons of his shirt, fumbling to push aside the fabric, exposing the skin beneath. He brushed her fingers aside and ripped the shirt off, buttons popping loose, pinging off the coffee table and wood flooring.

Her laughter warmed the air, her smile lighting the room. "I could have unbuttoned that and saved you a tailoring bill."

"Damn the buttons," he growled. He leaned on one arm, working the rivet on her short denim skirt. When he had no luck pushing it through the hole, he shoved the skirt up over her hips and ripped her panties down to her ankles.

"Hey, big guy. You may have a tailor on retainer. I don't."

"I'll buy you new ones." He jerked the fabric, the delicate lace ripping into shreds.

JOLIE LAY AGAINST THE SOFT leather couch, her breathing coming in ragged gulps, her body on fire, her skin deliciously sensitized to the cool air and warm fingers splayed out over her belly.

For six years she'd secretly imagined being naked with her boss. Fantasized about making love to him, his hands smoothing down over her body, his words of adoration and passion igniting her senses.

The reality was so much different than the dream. So much more vibrant, raw and exciting. She pulled at the belt around his middle, slipped the button loose on his suit trousers and slid the zipper down.

He sprang free, his erection long, thick and hot in her palm.

Her fingers curled around him and she stroked him, reveling in the sexy length of steel encased in velvet.

His body stiffened and he withdrew from her hands. "Not yet."

She transferred her fingers to his torso, sliding up his chest as he moved down over her body, his lips blazing a path from her breasts, skipping over the wadded skirt to her navel and lower still.

Devin's fingers found the patch of curls at the juncture of her thighs, parting the folds hiding beneath. When he touched her there, she gasped, her bottom rising up to meet his caress, her nerves on fire, her blood burning through every vein.

He flicked a finger over that sensitive nub, diving lower to delve into the warm moisture of her core.

"Oh, yes," she whispered. This was so much better than any fantasy. So much more intense. All logic fled, the cool, collected executive assistant she'd been for six years dissolved into the seething inferno of molten heat. Her hand cupped his, pressing him deeper.

He stroked in and out, dragging her juices up to the center of her pleasure, gently teasing her to the very edge of sanity, pushing her past any defenses she'd so carefully erected between boss and employee.

She couldn't remember her name, much less why this wasn't a good idea. All Jolie could do was live for the next moment, the next touch of his fingers, his lips, the broad length of his erection.

Intense sensations built to a crescendo, spilling from her core to flood throughout her body. She jerked, writhed and called his name aloud as she clung to his arms, her fingers digging into his skin.

Still riding the wave of lust, she wanted him inside her, to fill her, complete her. With desperate hands, she dragged him closer.

He nudged her legs apart and slid between them.

Jolie cupped his staff and guided him to her opening, slick with her juices.

With the tip of his shaft pressing into her, he paused. "We can't."

Jolie whimpered, too entrenched in passion to understand what he was saying. "What?"

"Not without protection."

"Oh." Her fingers shook against his chest. "Do you have some?" She didn't, and her body didn't give a damn about it at this point. Every nerve ending screamed for him to ram into her, damn the consequences.

He lurched to his feet, let his trousers slide the rest of the way to the ground. Finally naked.

Jolie's mouth went dry. Every fantasy she'd had of him naked didn't come close to the stunning reality.

He was a Greek god, his body tanned, toned and rippling with muscles.

With her skirt bunched around her middle, her legs open and her hair in wild disarray around her head, self-doubt flooded her. How could a man who looked like that even consider making love to a toadstool like her?

She sat up, drawing her legs together, pushing her skirt down over her crotch. "I'm sorry. I shouldn't have gotten so carried away." Jolie pushed to her feet, her arms crossing over her bare breasts, her gaze avoiding his, as she attempted to locate her missing bra.

His hands descended on her shoulders, forcing her to look up at him. "Don't tell me you're getting cold feet now." He sucked in a deep breath, closing his eyes. "You're so beautiful that I'm about to explode."

"Me?"

"Yes, you." His fingers slid down over her arms and his hand guided her hand to his member. "I didn't get this way just because. You're my inspiration."

"I am?" For a well-spoken executive assistant, she sounded like a complete idiot. Jolie didn't care. The words he spoke warmed her inside and out.

His eyebrows drew together. "But if you want me to stop, I will." He ran his free hand through his hair and dragged in another deep breath. "I don't know how, but I will. Just say the word."

She stared up into his eyes, her normal emerald-green gaze as dark as a primeval forest. Then her fingers tightened around his girth and she stepped closer. "Don't stop now."

He let out a sharp stream of air, bent and scooped her into his arms.

Caught off guard, she squealed, loving the feel of his naked body against her skin. He strode across the wide expanse of his living room and through a door into a spacious bedroom. Centered against one wall stood a king-size bed. Without pausing, he closed the distance between the door and the bed in five long strides. There he set her on her feet and he reached into the nightstand, removing a strip of foil packages.

His gaze turned feral, his mouth tilting upward at the corners. "I hope I have enough."

Jolie laughed shakily as she unbuttoned her skirt, her fingers twisting in the fabric, suddenly shy about standing in front of him with nothing on. She was so darned plain and pale, not tanned and beautiful like the rich crowd he hung around with.

His gaze captured hers and he tossed the condoms to the bed. "Lose it."

"Pardon?" She glanced up at him, her breath caught in her throat.

"The skirt." He gripped the waistband, his blue eyes darkening to smoky gray. "On second thought, let me."

Jolie lifted her hands out of the way as Devin slid the skirt down over her hips, dropping to his knees in front of her. He guided her backward until the backs of her legs touched the bed and she sat.

Still on his knees, Devin moved in between her thighs and draped them over his shoulder.

Incapable of breathing, Jolie's eyes widened and she watched as he trailed kisses along the tender insides of her thighs. When his mouth reached her center, his tongue thrust inside her.

She gasped and fell back against the duvet, a barrage of electrical shocks originating from where he touched her and shooting to every cell in her body.

He licked his way up to the sensitive nub, sucking it into his mouth and pulling gently. Large, warm fingers slid inside her, first two, then three.

Jolie writhed and twisted against the mattress, her own fingers digging into his hair, dragging him closer.

As far as she was concerned, she'd died and floated to heaven, the rise to the top a sharp climb. When she pitched over the edge, she drifted away into an abyss of pleasure so intense the rest of the world no longer existed.

Devin rose to his feet, wrapped her legs around his waist and thrust into her. With his hands holding her hips, he settled into a breath-catching rhythm, riding her until his body stiffened. He threw back his head and roared her name.

Jolie couldn't remember a man ever roaring her name aloud while making love. The experience was phenomenal and extremely erotic.

As they both returned to earth, Jolie scooted back on the bed until her head rested against the pillows.

Devin slid in beside her, his hand cupping a breast. Within minutes he slipped into a deep sleep.

Her body still quaking with energy, Jolie couldn't relax. If Devin was awake, she'd demand a repeat performance. But the poor man hadn't slept in days. She couldn't bear to wake him just for a little more of the most explosively satisfying sex she'd ever had.

As Jolie lay in the shadows, she studied Devin's face, tranquil in slumber. In some ways he looked like a little lost boy; in other ways, he could never be mistaken for little or lost, or a boy for that matter.

For six long years, Jolie had dreamed of just such a night with the boss. Now that she'd lived the dream what was she supposed to do? Lie there until morning and suffer the embarrassment of the morning-after? What if he regretted making love to her? What if this brief, powerful interlude ruined their working relationship?

As she lay there with Devin's hand warm against her breast, every scenario she could imagine pinged around her brain. Each outcome was worse than the last.

Before long, she'd talked herself into a mild panic attack, one thing forging through her tumbled thoughts. She had to get out of his condo. The sooner the better.

With a long look at the man she'd loved since the first day she came to work for him, Jolie slid from the bed and gathered her things. She slung her clothing on in the living room of the warehouse condo, not taking the time to button and zip her jean skirt. Her panties were ruined, so she'd have to go commando until she reached her apartment.

Mostly dressed and eager to leave without waking Devin, Jolie slipped out the door a little after midnight.

At the bottom of the staircase leading up to his condo, she turned toward the parking lot, pausing briefly to zip and button her skirt.

A bright light flashed in her eyes and she squealed, throwing up her hands to shield her face from further attack.

"Thanks, lady!" A man carrying a mammoth camera ran across the road and jumped into a car parked illegally against the curb. Before Jolie's night vision recovered, he was gone.

Her heart plummeting into her belly, she hurried toward her car. "Damned paparazzi."

Tomorrow there would be hell to pay.

Chapter Three

Jolie spent the rest of the night pacing the floor of her small apartment, nestled in a tight little community a few miles away from Devin's condo. Definitely in a lower rent district.

She'd tried to sleep but as soon as she lay against the sheets, she remembered lying next to Devin, curled against his side, his body warm and naked. Her skin heated, her breathing grew unsteady and a rush of lust washed over her. Sleep had been impossible.

Now that she'd done the deed with the boss, she had decisions to make. Normally a methodical person, used to order and structure in her life, Jolie found that she couldn't focus for ten seconds on anything.

After the twentieth lap around her couch, she stopped in front of the wall and banged her head against the textured paint. "What have I done?"

A simple gesture of concern had turned into one of the biggest mistakes of her life. And yet, she couldn't totally regret what had happened. She'd always wanted to know what it would be like to make love to Devin Kendall. She just didn't want to lose her job over it. Losing her job meant never seeing Devin again. She'd rather love him from the distance of his office to hers than from somewhere completely out of sight and mind.

She also liked working for Kendall Communications. The company was headed in exciting new directions and she enjoyed being a part of the growth. Jolie loved the fast-paced environment of managing the CEO's schedule. She'd made the necessary sacrifices to get where she was, going to school at night, paying her own way through business school and then crafting the winning résumé that landed her with Devin as his executive assistant.

If she left Kendall Communications, where would she go to work? And if word got out that she was fired for sleeping with the boss, who would hire her?

What a mess.

Ten laps later, she checked the clock over the microwave. One hour before she should be getting up, anyway. She might as well get ready for work and start early. Maybe she could get the email, snail mail and the day's in-box in order before Devin walked into the office.

If their changed relationship didn't work out, she'd have to move on. She wondered if Devin would give her a recommendation and almost laughed at how it might read. "Very organized, efficient office manager and great in bed."

God, how was she going to face him this morning?

She strode into the bathroom, stripped and climbed into the shower.

Water sluiced over her body, warm and wet, like she'd been when he'd thrust into her. She rubbed soap over her skin, her hands sinking low to the juncture of her thighs, that sore and achy place that…

Argh! Why couldn't she block it from her mind? She decreased the flow of warm water until what came out of the nozzle was bone-jarringly cold. By the time she climbed from the tub, her skin had shriveled into a landscape of goose bumps.

Jolie dug through her closet for her most boring and nondescript suit. It didn't take long for her to find one. They were all boring and nondescript. Soft gray or navy blue, with a classic design that would never go out of fashion or truly be considered fashionable for that matter.

She dug deeper, looking for anything different and came up empty. Why would she care to look better, anyway? Devin wasn't interested in what she wore, and the sooner they got back to business as usual, the better.

Jolie had worked hard to become the perfect executive assistant. She was all about cool, quiet efficiency. Then why were her nerves frayed and her hands shaking as she slipped her skirt up over her hips? The same hips Devin had slid his hands over while undressing her....

She ran a brush through her hair and started to pull it back into the usual elegant chignon she wore, but her hands froze as she peered at herself in the mirror.

Her cheeks were flushed, her eyes bright, and she looked markedly different. At the last moment, she decided to leave her hair hanging down around her shoulders.

Devin had noticed her hair. He'd said she looked softer, more personable.

And why should she let that influence the way she wore her hair? With quick, skillful twists, she had her hair up and ready for another day at the office. Looking normal was half the battle when her insides were turning cartwheels.

Ready an hour early, Jolie rationalized that she could get a lot done while no one was there to interrupt. In truth, she didn't want to run the gauntlet of company staff on her way to the executive suite. She could slip in, hang low and weather this storm.

Jolie smoothed her skirt, breathed in deeply and, as

she let the air out of her lungs, opened her front door. As usual, her morning paper lay against the steps, rolled with a rubber band around it. She tucked it beneath her arm and headed for work.

Cool, calm, collected. She could do this.

LOUD BANGING WOKE DEVIN. He blinked his eyes open and stared at the triangle of light shining through the crack in the curtains. It took a full ten seconds to dawn on him that it was morning.

Morning. Not a weekend morning, either. Sweet Jesus, he must have actually slept. His gaze shot to the alarm clock on his nightstand and he leaped out of bed. It was well past time to get up. He'd be late for work by at least an hour.

The banging started again and he realized someone was knocking at the door to his condo. "Hold on, I'm coming," he yelled, pulling on the trousers he'd worn the night before and zipping as he strode through the living room.

The banging increased in intensity until Devin grabbed the door handle and flung it open. "Where's the fire?"

Ash slapped something at his chest and brushed past him into the condo. "Shut the door."

Devin shook his head. "Good morning to you, too."

"Can the sarcasm. We have a problem."

"We?"

"Not really we. You."

"Me?" Devin shook his head in an attempt to dislodge the last remnants of sleep.

Ash kept walking until he reached the kitchen where he rifled through the cabinets, slamming them one at a time. "Where's your damned coffee? I can't function without coffee."

"Next to the coffeemaker." Devin followed, his eyebrows dipping downward. "What are you talking about?"

Ash sprinkled coffee grains into the filter and poured water into the well. "I take it you haven't seen the newspaper this morning?"

Devin glanced down at the front page Ash had shoved at him. Jolie's surprised face stared back at him, her hands poised at the bottom of her open zipper, the smooth flesh of her belly clearly visible to the camera. His breath caught in his chest as if he'd been sucker punched. "What the hell?"

"Read the caption." Ash switched the coffeemaker on and crossed his arms over his chest. "It gets better."

Sex Kitten Buttons Up After Leaving Kendall Communications CEO. Devin swore and would have ripped the paper to shreds, but Ash stopped him.

"Keep reading." He pointed to the second paragraph. "Apparently this guy was there when Jolie arrived and waited until she left. He even noted that she was more disheveled when she left." Ash pointed to the paragraph and read aloud, "'Devin Kendall seeks sensual stress relief while the Christmas Eve Murders case smolders. What role did he play in the demise of his parents and what does the CEO really do behind closed doors in his office? Board members have a right to know.'"

Devin shoved a hand through his hair. "Damn." Jolie would be devastated. She prided herself on her professionalism.

"I can't believe you weren't more circumspect. Especially with the ongoing murder investigation. You had to know the reporters would be staking us out even more than usual."

Devin shoved a hand through his hair. "I know, I know."

"Then why?"

"I don't know," Devin shouted, his head beginning to pound. He slammed the paper on the counter and paced barefoot across the length of the kitchen. "Where is Jolie now?"

"She's at work. She called me when you didn't show up on time."

"Why didn't she call me?" Devin muttered. "I can't believe I overslept. I'll be ready to go in five minutes and we'll get this mess straightened out." He headed for the bedroom.

"I don't see how. The damage is done."

"I'll fix it, I tell you." He had to. Jolie would not be happy about being splashed across the newspaper. The paparazzi would make something sordid out of what had been…well, the best sex he'd had in forever.

Hell, it had been more than that, but right now Devin couldn't think past Jolie's reaction to the news. He had to get to her quickly. Together they'd come up with a solution that would keep Kendall Communications from being dragged through the mud.

God, he'd been through enough media trashing to know where this was headed. As one of the most eligible bachelors in St. Louis and the CEO of Kendall Communications, the news reporters jumped at any chance to rake him over the coals.

The last woman he'd had a relationship with had given the media months of fodder. They'd hounded the poor woman, calling her every tawdry name in the book until she'd been forced to leave St. Louis altogether.

Devin's jaw hardened. With the murder investigation reopened, he couldn't afford to let the media drag the Kendalls or Jolie down into the gutter.

More importantly, they'd have to do something to keep

Jolie from being labeled a gold digger, a kept woman or worse. She deserved better. She hadn't come on to him, he'd come on to her.

After four minutes in the shower beneath the icy-cold spray, Devin had come up with a plan. His family might not like the suddenness of his announcement, but he had to do it to avoid the media circus an untimely affair would generate.

Ash followed him through the streets of St. Louis in his own car, arriving seconds later as he parked in one of the spaces reserved for executive staff.

They rode the elevator together in silence, up to the twenty-fourth floor.

Heads turned as they walked by office doors where people milled around in the aisles. Devin glared at anyone who dared to speak to him or whisper as he passed.

When he reached his suite of offices, he breezed past Jolie, who didn't even look at him, or attempt to say good morning as was the usual greeting she'd dished out every day for the past six years.

Yeah, Devin had really screwed things up royally this time. But he'd fix it. He had a plan.

When he reached his office, he turned and barked, "Jolie! In here." Okay, so that wasn't exactly how he'd planned to start this conversation, but he was so mad at himself he couldn't take the edge off his anger enough to be civil.

Jolie grabbed a steno pad and ducked around him into his office, her cheeks flaming a bright pink.

Staff foolish enough to be standing within sight were the recipients of Devin's harshest glare. "There are a hundred people who want your jobs. I suggest you get to work." With that he started to slam his door, but Ash got in his way.

"Move it or lose it," Devin threatened.

"The entire family has a stake in this."

"Not now. This is between me and Jolie." If Devin could have breathed fire onto his brother, he would have.

Ash saw it and relented. "Make it quick, we have to conduct some serious damage control. I'm going to get Uncle Craig and Natalie."

Devin closed the door in his brother's face and turned to Jolie. His chest tightened as he took in her prim and proper appearance. No one would ever look at her like this again. Especially him. All he could picture was her lying naked across his bed.

The public would forever see the woman on the front page, whose hair had curled around her face and whose lips looked swollen from a marathon of kissing. What had she done to deserve the wrong kind of attention?

She'd been kind to him. That's what. And he'd taken advantage of her.

"If this is about the newspaper, I'm sorry. I didn't know that photographer was there when I left last night. I didn't even think about it. I was in a hurry to—"

Devin raised his hand to stop her ramble. Jolie never rambled. She chose her words with care. Damn, she'd been more disturbed than he'd thought by what had happened. "This isn't your fault. I don't blame you for what happened. In fact, all the blame goes to me."

She shook her head, her mouth forming her next argument.

"Let me finish." Devin walked across to her and gripped her shoulders. "I shouldn't have taken advantage of you when you'd been good enough to bring me food." His voice sounded formal, stiff and so different from what he wanted to sound like for the next thing he had to say. "I should never have kissed you." And dear God, he wanted to kiss her again. Another mistake getting this close to her after last night.

She stared up at him, her eyes limpid pools of green. "I shouldn't have kissed you back." She swayed toward him, her gaze dropping to his mouth.

Ah, hell, he knew where this was going and was powerless to stop himself. "I can fix this…." His head dipped and he claimed her lips, his own slanting down over hers, crushing her to him.

His fingers slid up the back of her neck into the smooth twist, loosening the pins until the long tresses fell down around her shoulders.

She didn't seem to notice, her tongue slipping through his teeth to stroke his. Her hands climbed his chest and circled behind his neck, pulling him closer.

A knock on the door brought Devin back to earth with a jolt. "Just a minute." He pushed her to arm's length and sucked in a breath, trying to focus on what he had to say next, not on how much he wanted to kiss her again. "What's done is done. What I don't want to happen is for the media to drag the Kendall family down during this murder investigation. Nor do I want them to turn on you and ruin your reputation."

Jolie raised shaking hands to her hair, pushing it back behind her ears. "I understand. Would it be better if I quit? I could formally announce my resignation if that would help."

"No." He said the one little word with more emphasis than he'd intended. The thought of losing a wonderful executive assistant because of his indiscretion made him want to hit someone. Himself, if he could. "I have an entirely different proposal for you."

She tipped her head, eyebrows dipping low on her pale forehead. "Proposal?"

His lips quirked up on the edges, the irony of his word choice striking him as unfortunately funny. "Since I dragged you into our family troubles, the least I can do is deflect the drama from last night's…assignation."

"And how are you going to do that?"

"By announcing our engagement."

Chapter Four

Jolie staggered backward, pulling free of his grasp, her head spinning. When the backs of her knees hit the wing-backed chair, she sat down hard, a hand rising to her cheek. She couldn't breathe, her heart having stopped at Devin's words. "Engagement?" Had her every dream just come true?

"It's the only way we can salvage the situation and deflect the media inquisition." He turned and paced the floor. "It will be a fake engagement, of course. I won't expect you to go through with the marriage."

Jolie's gut roiled as if she'd been punched hard. Blood rushed back into her face and her heart surged into gear. She clutched her hands together in her lap, her gaze on her fingers, not Devin, as she forced her disappointment aside. Why had she even dared to believe a man like Devin would be interested in marrying a girl like herself? *Fool.*

They were worlds apart. While Devin dined on caviar and two-hundred-dollar steaks, she cooked her own meals and ate leftovers. Not that she didn't make good money as the CEO's assistant, she just didn't have the kind of income to throw away on extravagance.

Devin faced her directly. "Fake only to you and me. The rest of the family must believe it's true in order to convince the paparazzi."

"Don't you think they deserve to know the truth?" Jolie asked, glad his focus was on his family and not her. It gave her time to think through her response.

"They will be safer with the lie. That way only the two of us will have to keep up the pretense, limiting the number of people who could slip, blowing our story. It keeps the rest of the family from worrying about making the wrong move or saying the wrong thing."

Jolie stood. "And if I'm not willing to participate in this lie?"

"Why wouldn't you? It's to protect you from a media nightmare and Kendall Communications from a scandal. We keep the focus on something exciting, like a wedding. And not that our family is being investigated regarding the murders. That way, we can continue our own investigation without being too obvious."

She swallowed hard, a wad of tears clogging her throat. Oh, dear God, don't let her cry in front of him. Devin hated when women cried. She turned her back to him. "I think it would be best if I quit." How could she see Devin day in and day out and not fall more hopelessly in love? Especially after the previous night's indiscretions?

The carpeted floor muted Devin's approach, but every nerve in Jolie's body knew he'd closed the distance between them. When his hands descended on her shoulders, she sucked in a breath and held it.

Devin turned her to face him. "The media will crucify you and me if you quit now. I don't care about me, but I don't want you hurt because of my mistake." He pulled her into his arms.

Mistake. Jolie held herself stiff. What they'd done last night was a mistake to him. She let the air out of her lungs and steeled her voice not to shake, as she responded, "I'm tough, I won't break. Besides, how can we work together now that we've done…what we've done?" *The mistake*.

"I could promise not to touch you again, but I hate breaking promises." He tipped her chin up with his thumb. "Do it for me. Be my fiancée. When the hoopla dies down we can break the engagement and everything can go back to normal." His blue-eyed gaze bored into hers. His thick brown hair fell down over his forehead as though he hadn't taken the time to tame it that morning, making him appear more vulnerable.

When he looked at her like that, how could she resist? Damn, she was a mess. "Okay, I'll do it. But when this ordeal is over, we have to face reality."

"We will. Later." His lips tipped upward at the corner. "Ash is gathering the family. I wish Thad was here, but that can't be helped. We can announce our engagement to them now to quell their uproar at the morning news."

Jolie nodded and forced herself to smile. "I guess we're engaged. Sort of." Her laugh sounded stiff, even to her own ears. "Somehow, I pictured my first proposal differently." She shrugged, maintaining her pretense of nonchalance when what she really wanted was to find a quiet, dark closet to hide in until her insides quit trembling. She could just imagine her reaction had it been a real engagement.

A long silence stretched between them, with Devin's hands still resting on her arms.

Jolie's gaze collided with Devin's intense blue eyes.

He stared into her face, his forehead wrinkled as it did when he was working out a problem in his head.

"What?" She crossed her eyes in an attempt to view the tip of her nose. "Do I have a smudge on my face?"

"No. It's just…"

"Having second thoughts?" Her heart stuttered to a

stop and she held her breath. Not like the engagement was real or anything. "That's bad when you're having second thoughts about a fake engagement. Does the thought of a Kendall marrying a lowly executive assistant go against the grain?" She tried to laugh, failing miserably.

"Huh?" He shook his head. "No, don't be silly. I was thinking we should seal this deal in some way." His frown lifted and he leaned closer, his hand rising to cup the back of her neck, drawing her closer. "Perhaps with a kiss."

Jolie leaned forward, memories of the night before rushing in to fuel the flames building inside. Her breasts touched his chest, the hardened tips rubbing deliciously against the inside of her lacy bra.

Her arms crept up and around his neck, pulling him closer.

Devin's lips crushed her mouth, his tongue sweeping in to tangle with hers, thrusting and tempting her to forget everything but that moment.

A professional down to the sensible shoes she wore, Jolie had been thrown into the deep end. Kissing the boss in his office wasn't something a woman did, unless that woman was completely out of her mind in love.

A sound penetrated the back of her thoughts, the creak of a door opening, the light squeal of a hinge.

"Oops, sorry, didn't mean to interrupt."

Jolie jumped back, her eyes wide, her heart thumping against her ribs.

Natalie stood at the door, her face flushed, her green eyes dancing. "I can come back when you've concluded your…er…meeting."

"Bull on that." Ash pushed his way through the door, followed by the owner and one of the original cofounders of Kendall Communications, Craig Kendall. "We have some serious damage control to conduct and you two aren't helping by playing tonsil tango on company time."

Her face burning, Jolie attempted a dash for the door.

Devin, anticipating her move, grabbed her arm and pulled her against him, his hand slipping around her waist. "I'm glad you were all able to join us on such short notice. I'm certain you have seen the morning newspaper?"

Every head nodded.

He stood straighter and faced curious eyes. "Well, I have an explanation for that."

"I'm glad someone does." Craig crossed his arms and waited. "Go on."

"Jolie and I have an announcement to make."

Natalie's eyes widened, her mouth falling open. "No way."

Devin glared at her. "I haven't even said what it is and you're already saying 'no way'?"

"No way!" Natalie clamped her mouth shut and slapped a hand over it. Through her fingers she muttered, "Okay, I won't say a word, oh, my God, hurry up with it."

A chuckle rose up in Devin's chest. "How old are you?"

Natalie dropped her hand. "Twenty-six, will you tell already?"

If Jolie didn't have a knot the size of a sweat sock lodged in her throat, she'd have laughed out loud at Natalie's enthusiasm. But the whole situation was surreal, as though it was happening to someone else. Not plain Jolie Carson.

Devin smiled down at Jolie and winked.

Immediately, her world lit and her nerves calmed. She could handle just about anything if Devin Kendall looked at her like that all the time.

"Jolie and I are engaged."

Natalie squealed and rushed forward to hug Jolie. "I knew it. I knew it."

"How did you know?" Ash asked, his gaze on Devin, not Natalie. "None of us knew until now, unless you had some inside information."

"Oh, Ash, relax." Natalie hugged Jolie and turned back to face her detective brother. "I could tell by the look on Jolie's face."

"What, the look of stunned disbelief?" Jolie pressed a hand to her burning cheeks. "I can barely believe it's true."

Natalie hugged her again. "I get another sister. I won't be outnumbered by men anymore."

Ash frowned at Devin. "That's the way you're going to play this?"

Devin met his frown with a clear and steady gaze. "We're not playing. Jolie and I are getting married."

"When?" Ash shot back at him.

Fighting to keep irritation from rising into his voice, Devin answered, "We haven't set a date."

"Ash." Natalie glared at her brother.

Ash refused to be quieted. "I want the truth."

Jolie's arm slipped around Devin's waist and she smiled up at him. "Devin just asked me to marry him. I haven't thought that far ahead. I've been pinching myself, thinking I'm still sleeping."

"I just don't want you two walking into something you'll both regret because of a picture in the newspaper."

"We should give the couple a little space." Uncle Craig winked, saving Devin from a response. "They have some…er…celebrating to do. Aunt Angela and I will help you with the wedding preparations. We can shop for two since Rachel and Ash will be getting married soon, too."

"Why don't you two get started?" Devin said.

Jolie chimed in, "Just because we're engaged doesn't mean I'm commitment free. I have a job to do and a very demanding boss."

Ash smiled for the first time since Devin's announcement. "I think you've met your match there, brother. How are you going to live without her managing your office?"

Devin frowned. "I hadn't thought about that."

"Because he's not going to live without me managing his office. At least not until I find a suitable replacement." Her arm dropped from around his waist and Jolie stepped back. "Now I have work to do."

Devin grabbed her hand to keep her from going too far. "You're officially off the clock at three this afternoon."

"I have too much to do to take off that early."

"You need time to find a new dress. Natalie will help you." He fished in his pocket for his wallet and withdrew a credit card. "You can use this."

Jolie's hands shot up. "No, really, I don't need a new dress."

"You do for tonight. It's a special occasion. We'll be attending the gala for the St. Louis Children's Hospital."

"I can wear the dress I wore to the company Christmas party," she insisted.

"No." Devin loved the mutinous expression on her face and wanted to kiss it off. But with his uncle, brother and sister watching, he held back, holding to the firm older brother and CEO persona. "You will buy a new dress." Devin pressed the credit card into her hand and curled her fingers around it. "And while you're at it, some new shoes. We're announcing our engagement to the city at the gala."

Jolie opened her mouth to protest, then shut it.

Devin almost laughed out loud. "What is it you always say?"

Jolie sighed. "Stop finding reasons not to and start finding reasons to." She scowled for a moment, then a smile curved her lips, making the entire office light up. "You're absolutely right. I think I'll take the rest of the day off. Finding the right dress could prove challenging." She turned to Natalie. "Can you spare the afternoon?"

"I don't know. Devin has my proposal for the advertising campaign. I believe Jolie delivered it last night. Or had you forgotten?" Natalie cocked an eyebrow at her brother. "Until you review it, I'm at loose ends. If you need me, I'll be out with your fiancée." She flung her hair over her shoulder, hooked her elbow through Jolie's and tugged her toward the door. "Come on, sister. We have some power shopping to do."

Devin's gaze followed them through the door, the scent of Jolie's perfume lingering in the air, reminding him of the hours they'd spent in his bed. Hell, his sheets still smelled of Jolie.

"If you two will excuse me, I have to prepare for the gala, as well. We're making a sizable donation to the hospital and I need to make sure Accounting has written the check." Uncle Craig stuck his hand out. "Congratulations, son."

Devin took his uncle's hand and was pulled into a bear hug.

Guilt gnawed at his insides. How could he lie to the people he loved about a matter like an engagement? But for their own protection, it had to be that way. "Thanks, Uncle."

As soon as the door closed behind his uncle, Devin braced himself for his brother's inquisition.

"Why?" Ash started.

Devin turned away from his brother and walked to the floor-to-ceiling windows overlooking the St. Louis skyline. The arch gleamed white in the morning sun, like a beacon of hope under the weight of the resurgence of the case of the Christmas Eve Murders. "I would think it obvious. We're in love."

Devin marveled at how easily the lie rolled off his lips. Not that he couldn't fall in love with Jolie. After last night, he truly believed he could. Why he hadn't seen it earlier was a mystery to him. Still, his responsibility to his family came first. His own desires had always gone on the back burner.

"As much as we all love and appreciate everything Jolie has done for you, I feel that the media is pushing you into this farce of an engagement."

Devin looked back over his shoulder. "Ash, have you ever known anyone to push me into doing something I didn't want to?"

Ash sighed. "No."

"Then leave it at that. Jolie and I are getting married. We make the news public tonight."

Ash dug his hands into his pockets and rocked back on his heels. "At the very least, your engagement will lay the wagging tongues to rest."

Devin nodded. "Any new forensic evidence surface?"

Ash shook his head. "You're changing the subject."

"No, the previous conversation was over."

Ash's lips twisted and then turned up in a smile. "Rachel and I have gone over and over the evidence remaining from twenty years ago. We've got nothing. No new matches have surfaced on the DNA in the National DNA Database. Which only tells us that whoever murdered our parents hasn't been convicted of another crime."

"Why would someone come after us now, when they've been safely hidden for all these years?"

"Could be a couple of reasons." Ash paced the carpeted floor. "The exoneration of the man originally charged with the murders could have shaken the real killer. He might want to eliminate all those who give a damn about our parents. He could be operating under the assumption that if no one is monitoring the case, it will grow cold again."

"Or it could be someone hoping to use the past murders as a cover."

Ash stopped pacing. "I'd thought of that, which is part of the reason I'm here today. I'm compiling a list of all those who hate the Kendalls and want us dead."

"That might take a while." Devin's lips twisted. "Anytime you own a big corporation, you're going to piss someone off."

"Start with disgruntled ex-employees. Work the inside first and anyone you might have fired in the past year. The reopening of the murder investigation gives someone an opportunity to hide behind an existing killer."

"I'll get Jolie on it." Devin reached for the intercom button on his phone.

His brother smiled. "Afraid that won't work."

Devin snatched his hand away. "Oh, yeah. She's shopping." He frowned. "How the hell am I supposed to function without her in the office?" he grumbled, staring down at his desk as if it was a foreign object.

"Guess you'll have to figure that one out on your own. If you can have that list to me by the end of the day, I'll get to work on background checks."

"Don't forget you'll be expected at the gala tonight."

"Why me?" Ash asked.

"Is your last name Kendall?"

"Yeah. So?" Ash crossed his arms over his chest. "I'm not part of Kendall Communications. I'm a cop."

"And a part of this family. You know we always attend this gala together. It's for the kids."

"I know, I'm just yanking your chain. Besides, if I don't take Rachel, she'll skin me alive. She wants to wear some kick-ass red dress she bought." Ash smiled. "Actually, I can't wait to see her in it." His grin turned wicked. "And out of it. On second thoughts, we might not make that gala after all."

"Make it." Devin gave Ash a stern look. "It's for the kids. And, who knows, maybe the killer will be there."

"Sure. I'll recognize him and arrest him on the spot." Ash laughed. "We can always dream." His smile faded. "Seriously, no one travels alone tonight. Got that?"

"I've arranged for two limos to take us all there. We'll pick up Jolie on the way."

"It's a date." Ash performed an about-face and headed for the door. When he reached it, he paused with his hand on the knob. "Don't forget the list of employees or business associates Kendall Communications has wronged over the past year."

"Yeah, yeah. Why don't you do your job and let me do mine." Devin waved his brother out.

As soon as the door closed behind Ash, Devin sat in his leather chair and stared at the neat stack of papers requiring his attention. Instead of getting to work on company business, he pulled out a pad and pen and went to work on who might be interested in seeing the Kendall family suffer or die.

After he'd listed the competition that had failed or that Kendall Communications had bought out over the past year, he paused. Could it be someone on the inside? Someone who knew when the Kendalls entered and exited the building?

Devin punched the intercom button but stopped when he realized Jolie wasn't there to answer.

Hell, Jolie was always there. The woman anticipated his every move and desire.

Devin's groin tightened.

She knew exactly what he liked, from the cinnamon in his coffee to the way she cried out when making love.

He slammed his hand onto his desk. Why the hell did he have to screw up a perfectly good office relationship? Yet, he couldn't regret what had happened the night before.

No. He couldn't regret it and definitely couldn't forget.

The anticipation of seeing Jolie decked out in a form-fitting evening gown had him eager for the day to end so that he could see her again, touch her skin, smell the perfume that lingered even when she'd left the room.

He stared at the list in front of him and sighed.

Making love with Jolie had done exactly what he'd avoided for the past twenty years. It had distracted his attention from his family and no matter what, he owed his family his utter devotion. Especially since he'd failed to be there when his parents had been murdered.

What Devin Kendall wanted had to wait.

Catching the Christmas Eve murderer had top billing on his priority list.

Chapter Five

"Try this one." Natalie handed her a slinky black number that was little more than a thin sheath.

"I can't wear that in public." Jolie pushed it away. "It'll show every bump, lump and imperfection I have."

Natalie gave a very unladylike snort. "As if you have any imperfections." She straightened the dressing room curtain and spoke from the other side. "Honey, you have a model's body. Why didn't you go into modeling?"

"Oh, please." Jolie stepped out in a long silver gown that covered everything from the tips of her toes up to the lobes of her ears. "I'm not tall enough."

"You're close enough. What are you, five feet nine inches?"

"Yes, but, I'm too skinny."

"Do you know how many runway divas have bulimia trying to get that skinny?"

"I can't eat enough." She tugged at where the material stretched tightly over her chest. "My boobs are too big for a model, and I'm plain."

"You'd be perfect for a lingerie model and you're not plain. Your beauty is classic."

Jolie stared at the mess of a silver dress. "I just don't see it. And I don't get why Devin wants to parade me around town."

Natalie rolled her eyes. "Are you kidding me?" She turned Jolie around and pushed her into the dressing room. "First of all, he's marrying you, and we know he wouldn't be doing that unless he loved you."

Jolie flinched behind the curtain. *Lie number one.* "He's delirious from lack of sleep."

"Second, you're smart and confident."

Jolie shrugged out of the silver dress, letting it fall to the floor. "I'm smart-mouthed and pushy, and I didn't grow up in the same social circle as your family."

Natalie poked her head in the dressing room, a frown marring her pretty forehead. "You think Devin cares?"

Jolie covered her naked breasts. "Shouldn't he?"

"Jolie Carson, are you a snob?" Natalie jerked the curtain closed.

"No, it's just I can't see how I could ever fit into the Kendall family. You are all larger than life."

"We're people, just like you. We put our pants on the same way. There's no magic and Devin is no Prince Charming, let me tell you. No, wait. I don't want you getting cold feet on me now. I'm determined to even the male-female Kendall odds. Here, try this one." Natalie shoved a green dress through the curtain. "And you're gorgeous. You just need the right clothes to show off your body."

"You can dress a pig in a pink tutu and she's still a pig."

"You're not a pig, and I'd never dress you in pink. Not with that red hair."

"Which is another flaw—"

"Shut up and put the dress on."

Jolie clamped her lips shut and hurried into the dress. The color complemented her pale skin instead of making her look sickly. But skin wasn't everything. This dress had to be perfect for tonight—the night all her fake dreams came true.

For a moment, Jolie wanted to stomp her foot and scream at how unfair fate could be. To give her the man she loved and yet not. She tugged the dress up over her hips and zipped it as far up the back as she could reach.

She had to hang on to it to keep it from falling off. For once the top had plenty of room for her and then some.

Jolie sighed and stepped out of the dressing room. The deep-forest-green strapless dress swooped low on her chest. She tugged at the fabric that exposed more of her breasts than it covered. "What's the use? I can't wear this. It doesn't have anything to hold it up and it has a long train, someone will trip on it, probably me."

"Oh. My. God." Natalie stared at Jolie's reflection, her jaw dropping low. "Oh, my God." She circled her once, careful to step over the train. And then circled again. "This is it. This is the dress." She looked around Jolie. "Where's the saleswoman?"

Jolie shook her head, holding up her hands in warning. "Don't even think it. I'm not showing up at a huge gala in a dress that could fall off me at any moment."

"Are you kidding?" Natalie reached behind Jolie and zipped the dress the rest of the way up. "See? Not only is it the perfect color, it's a perfect fit. This dress was made for you."

Jolie had to admit, with the zipper done up right, the dress remained in place. She raised her arms and wiggled her torso. No slippage and no embarrassing flashes of breasts. Still unconvinced, she stared at herself in the mirror.

"You look like Julia Roberts in *Pretty Woman,* only instead of red, the dress is green." Natalie pulled Jolie's long red hair up on top of her head, letting the curls spill down the back. "With your hair up like this, every man in the room will be panting after you."

Jolie pressed a hand over her cleavage. "I don't want every man in the room panting after me. Just one." *My fake fiancé.*

"Trust me, he'll be looking. And panting." Natalie grabbed her hand and hurried her through the boutique, snagging a saleswoman along the way to the shoe display. A Kendall on a mission, Natalie pressed Jolie into a chair. "My friend needs footwear with sparkle."

Jolie hid a smile as the saleswoman popped to attention. "Yes, Miss Kendall. I have a pair of rhinestone-studded slides that will be heavenly with that gown." The woman rushed through a doorway into the rear of the shop.

Jolie tugged at the dress, searching for a sales tag. "How much is this dress? Will it max out my credit card?"

Natalie slapped her hands gently. "You heard my brother, the dress is on his card. Besides, you don't want to know how much, and he can afford it."

"I can't let him buy my dress, we aren't married yet." And never would be. "It's a matter of pride. I went to night school while holding down two jobs to get an education. And ask anyone, I didn't sleep my way to the top. I've worked for what I've gotten."

Natalie leaned over and hugged Jolie. "I know. You really are too good for that brother of mine."

"That's not what I meant. I just like to pull my own weight in a relationship. I never want to be dependent on anyone."

"You want to love and be loved because of who you are, not a bank account, right?" Natalie's smile was sad. "You don't realize how much I envy you. I grew up in the media spotlight. I've had to suspect every man I've dated of gold digging."

"Really?" Jolie shook her head. "Why? You're beautiful. Any man would love you just for who you are."

"To some men, beauty is the size of your bank account." Natalie shrugged. "Just once, I'd like to be plain Natalie Smith, a regular person."

Jolie hugged her friend. "You could never be regular. You're too vibrant and full of life to be regular."

"Still, don't judge a Kendall by the pocketbook. We have feelings just like anyone else." Natalie squeezed her shoulders.

Jolie swallowed hard, for the first time in a long time feeling she had family. Real family. The thought swelled in her chest and made her feel so good she wanted to cry. Then the elation leached away as she remembered her imminent departure from Kendall Communications. When the engagement ended, she knew she'd have to resign.

"Here we are." The saleswoman sailed into the room carrying a pair of sparkling high-heeled sandals.

She dropped down to sit on the stool in front of Jolie and slid the delicate shoes onto Jolie's feet. "There. You're perfect." The woman stood and held out a hand for Jolie. Then she moved to the side as Jolie stared into the three-way mirror.

The heels made her even taller and forced her to stand straight or fall over.

"Wait until my brother gets a load of you in that. If he wasn't already in love with you, he'd fall hard and fast." Natalie grinned. "We'll take it." She shooed Jolie to the dressing room. "Hurry, we have an appointment at my salon for hair and nails."

"What? When did you have time to make that?"

Natalie laughed. "I already had one and promised to tip big if my stylist could squeeze you in at the same time."

Behind the curtain Jolie cringed. The dress was going

to set her back probably a couple paychecks; what would the salon do to her meager savings?

"Hand me the dress so I can get the saleswoman to bag it while you're dressing."

Jolie stepped out of the dress feeling like Cinderella when her coach changed back into a pumpkin. The stress of pretending was wearing on her. How would she continue the pretense without going crazy? She hefted the yards of smooth fabric and handed it through the curtain.

When she'd slipped back into her gray, serviceable work skirt and jacket, she felt more in control and emerged from the dressing room, pulling her wallet from her handbag.

Natalie stood at the door, a long dress bag hung over her shoulder and a shoe box tucked under her arm. "All set?"

"But…" Jolie stared at the saleswoman and back to Natalie. "You didn't."

"No, Devin did. Now come on or we'll be late."

Jolie hurried after Natalie and out onto the sidewalk, ready to argue the point.

Halfway to where they'd parked, Natalie came to an abrupt halt. "Did you see that?"

Intent on catching up with Natalie, Jolie didn't stop in time and bumped into the other woman. "See what?"

"That man, the one standing by the streetlight on the opposite corner." Natalie nodded her head toward the man. "It's him." She shoved the dress bag and shoe box into Jolie's arms. "Hold these."

"Natalie, no." Forced to take the dress and shoes, Jolie juggled to keep from dropping them as Natalie darted out into the busy St. Louis street.

Cars honked and tires squealed. A taxi screeched to a halt, but not fast enough. His front bumper barely clipped

Natalie in the thigh with just enough force to knock her to the ground.

Jolie screamed and threw the gown bag and shoe box to the sidewalk, racing out into the street after Natalie.

Natalie staggered to her feet. "I'm okay. It's all right. No harm, no foul."

The cab driver jumped out of his vehicle. "What the heck are you trying to do, get killed?"

Natalie swayed for a second then straightened, her head turning toward the corner where she'd spotted her shadow man. "Damn. He's gone."

Jolie slipped an arm around her and held her up. "We're getting you to a hospital."

"No way. Nothing's broken. I didn't hit my head. I'll have a helluva bruise on my right hip, but nothing that won't mend."

"I'll believe it when the doctor has a look at you."

"Can we do that after the hair appointment? You don't know how sensitive a stylist can be."

"Damn the stylist. We'll do our own hair and nails. Do you want me to take you to the hospital or should I call an ambulance? It's either that or I call your brother."

Natalie chewed her lip. As she stood in the middle of the street a crowd gathered and cars honked.

"At the very least, let's get you out of the street." Jolie slipped an arm around her friend and led her to the curb.

Once there, Natalie grabbed Jolie's hand. "You can't tell my brothers about me getting hit."

"And how are you going to explain a limp and the bruises? Am I supposed to make something up about shopping, a contact sport?" Jolie smiled. "Let's get you to a hospital and make sure nothing's broken. Then we'll talk."

"Promise you won't tell Devin?"

"Promise me you won't run out in the street in front of a car again?"

Natalie grinned. "Promise."

Jolie grabbed the fallen dress and shoe box from the ground. Then hooking Natalie's elbow through hers, she herded her to her car, carefully avoiding actually wording promises of any kind. She'd have a talk with Devin to see if this new stalker was a bodyguard. Especially if Natalie was going to be foolish enough to go after him.

"WHAT DO YOU MEAN ALL THE women are at Jolie's?" Devin demanded.

Ash shrugged. "Rachel called me earlier and said she and Aunt Angela were headed that way and to pick them up there. I think it's some kind of girl bonding time."

Uncle Craig sat in the corner, a smile on his face. "I can't believe you're getting married. I thought you were married to the company."

"My engagement will not change the way I feel about Kendall Communications. I'm still the same man, the same CEO."

Uncle Craig nodded, crossing his arms over his chest. "The mighty Devin has finally succumbed."

Devin glared across at his uncle, refusing to defend himself. Even if the engagement was real and he was marrying Jolie, it wouldn't change his work habits or his dedication to the company.

Ash snorted. "Yeah, and you didn't arrive late for work this morning, either. Finding the one makes you reevaluate and reconsider the amount of time you spend on the job and away from her."

Uncle Craig grinned. "In this case, he won't be away from his wife. Jolie will be working alongside him."

"Then the door to his office will be shut more often."

Ash smirked. "I imagine he'll find it hard to keep his hands off her, having her around all the time."

"Unless he plans on finding another executive assistant. In which case he really should start recruiting now. It takes a while to find one as good as Miss Carson."

Devin's fists clenched. "Excuse me, I happen to be in the same vehicle. You can stop talking as though I'm not here." He took a deep calming breath and continued. "First of all, I'm not in the market for a new executive assistant. And second of all, I have the class—more, apparently, than the two of you—to keep my bedroom antics in the bedroom, not the office." He held up a hand. "Can we discuss the case?"

"You take the fun out of teasing, brother." Ash's smile faded. "I've looked over Uncle Craig's list and haven't found anyone that stands out. Still, I'll be making some visits and calls to verify. What did you find while drafting yours?"

"There were only two companies we bought out over the last year. We cleaned house, then assimilated them under the Kendall Communications umbrella, helping place those who lost their positions. An after-action survey indicated all were satisfied. None stood out as disgruntled."

"What about recently fired or laid-off KC employees?"

"We parted ways with ten employees. I spoke with friends of theirs and all seemed happily employed elsewhere or moved out of state." Devin dug a folded paper from his pocket and handed it to Ash. "As far as I could tell, nothing stood out."

"I'll check into these and see if I can dig up anything."

"When will you make the announcement about your engagement?" Uncle Craig asked.

"I don't know, what do you suggest?" Devin hadn't

thought that far ahead, only knowing he had to announce it early to keep Jolie from suffering a media inquisition.

"You don't want to take away too much from the purpose of the gala, that being to raise money for the children's hospital. I suggest you make a discreet announcement when we arrive and ask all questions to wait until another time."

Devin nodded. "We'll see," he said, choosing to keep his options open.

"Did you get a ring?" his uncle asked.

Devin's lips pressed into a line. "Not yet. I had several jewelers into my office this afternoon, but nothing seemed right."

His uncle shook his head. "You can't announce an engagement without a ring on her finger." His uncle smiled. "I figured you had enough to worry about, so I took it upon myself to come up with a backup plan."

"Oh?" Devin leaned forward.

Uncle Craig pulled a small box from his pocket and opened it. "This was my mother's, your grandmother's, ring. As the oldest Kendall heir, it belongs to you."

Devin pulled the ring from the box and stared down at it. A dark green emerald sparkled up at him in the overhead light. The surrounding diamonds shone, enhancing the beauty of the emerald. "Jolie's eyes are this color of green." After all the diamond rings he'd viewed that afternoon, he hadn't considered the colored gems, specifically the emerald. "It's perfect."

"Your grandmother would have wanted you to have it. She and your grandfather had a long and loving marriage. I like to think the ring brings luck to the bride who wears it."

"My parents' marriage wasn't long and loving. They argued constantly, from what I could remember." Devin turned the ring, letting the light shine off it in different directions.

His uncle sat back, his face impassive. "Your mother didn't want the ring, choosing a new diamond solitaire instead." He stared out the window at the city lights of St. Louis. "Your parents married for all the wrong reasons. You don't have to repeat their mistakes."

Devin sat back in his seat, his focus on the ring, his mind on his uncle's words, the lie of his engagement weighing heavily on his conscience. Almost as heavily as his guilt over his parents' deaths.

"This must be it," Ash announced.

"Good, the other limo is already there." Uncle Craig didn't wait for the chauffeur to open his door. He got out, rounded the vehicle and waited for Devin and Ash.

A light flickered off in an upstairs apartment.

Before Devin reached the front entrance to the building, his sister Natalie emerged carrying a long mink-brown cape. Her cream off-the-shoulder gown fell in satiny layers all the way to the ground. She looked like their mother, with her blond hair swept up in a smooth chignon, her carriage regal and elegant.

The way Natalie graced them with a gentle smile made Devin's heart swell with pride and love for his little sister. He'd do anything for her.

She limped slightly as she walked toward them. "About time you arrived."

"We're right on time." Devin frowned down at her legs. "Why are you limping?"

Natalie ducked her head and hurried past him, muttering, "Fell shopping."

Ash's fiancée, Rachel, appeared in the entrance, carrying her long black coat, a grin on her face. Her vivid red dress fit every inch of her curves snugly, her high heels

giving her petite body added height. She made straight
for Ash, leaning up on her toes to kiss him on the lips.
"Miss me?"

Ash growled and kissed her hard, his arm cinching her
to him in a territorial grip.

Devin envied the ease with which Ash and Rachel ex-
changed the kiss. Everything Devin and Jolie did would
be in support of the lie they'd told his family. He hoped
he could keep it up for the sake of those he loved.

Aunt Angela was next. She hurried forward carrying a
faux-fur stole over her arm. "You aren't going to recognize
Jolie. She's amazing."

Devin shifted impatiently. How could he not recognize
the woman who'd worked for him for the past six years?
What was all the fuss over a party dress, anyway? Still,
his pulse quickened as Jolie stepped through the door.

She hesitated on the landing, the light over the porch
shining softly down over her, picking up the coppery high-
lights in her luxurious red hair.

Devin's heart skipped a beat. He'd never seen her look
so elegant. Her hair was swept to one side, lying in loose,
touchable curls down over her bare shoulder. The style
showed off the long graceful line of her neck, a neck he
desperately wanted to kiss.

As his gaze swept downward over the swell of her
breasts, his groin tightened. Holy smokes, was it legal to
be that…exposed in public?

Ash surfaced from kissing Rachel long enough to emit
a long, low wolf call.

Devin shot a quelling glare at his brother, his attention immediately returning to the woman standing in the
doorway.

"Come on. Let them have their space," Natalie whispered.

Devin barely heard her or noticed the rest of the Kendalls moving toward the waiting limousines.

He stood transfixed, unable to believe his eyes. Was this really Jolie? The one-woman office dynamo? The completely professional executive assistant who managed to facilitate boardroom meetings, make damned good coffee and write memos that could make a businessman weep? Aunt Angela had been right. He didn't recognize her and she was amazing.

Jolie stepped down off the porch and moved toward him, a smile curving her lips. She stopped in front of him and touched a finger to the bottom of his chin. "You're making me nervous, standing there with your mouth open. Kiss me so your family thinks this is for real."

He didn't hesitate. His arms came up around her as if of their own accord. Devin claimed her lips, crushing her against him in a hold that dared someone to break it. His tongue swept past her teeth, delving in to taste her freshness, the warm wetness, a hint of what they'd shared the night before.

He forgot that he stood on the curb in view of his entire family. Forgot this was a display of the farce he'd concocted to deflect negative attention from the Kendalls and Jolie. He lived in the moment of kissing this stranger he'd completely missed for the past six years.

When they came up for air, Jolie laughed breathlessly and pressed a hand to her hair. Her eyes shone brightly and her cheeks flushed a soft pink. "Well, that should fool them."

Devin blinked and looked around to see his family climbing into the waiting limousine.

Uncle Craig held the door for the others. He shot a glance at Devin and pointed to his own ring finger.

Oh, yeah.

Jolie's gaze followed the others as the doors closed and the limo waited silently at the curb. "Shouldn't we be going?"

"In a minute." Nervous for the first time in a decade, Devin fumbled in his pocket for the ring his uncle had given him. "I have something for you."

Where was it? Finally he found the right pocket. His fingers closed around the ring and he pulled it out, keeping it tucked into his palm. He cast a glance at the waiting vehicle, certain all noses would be pressed against the tinted windows.

He cleared his throat. "First of all, let me tell you how incredibly remarkable you look tonight."

Jolie blushed and dipped her head. "You won't think it so amazing when you see the bill." Her head came up, her chin lifting defiantly. "Which, by the way, I intend to pay you back. Every cent."

He pressed a finger to her soft lips. "I won't let you, so don't bother."

The little crease in her forehead made Devin want to kiss it smooth.

He laughed. "I don't deserve you, Jolie. I don't know how to go about this properly and I know it's not for real, but here goes." He dropped to one knee and held her hand in his, the ring poised in front of her ring finger. He stared up into her eyes, feeling as if the world had ground to a halt waiting for what was next.

His tone low, his words soft and insistent, he spoke, "Jolie Carson, will you wear this ring and be my fake fiancée?"

Chapter Six

Jolie's smile slipped a bit as she blinked back the moisture in her eyes. She wanted to laugh and cry all at the same time. Instead, she tugged at the hand he held. "We've already been over this. I agreed to help out. Why ask again?"

Devin held tightly to her hand, refusing to let go. "You need a ring on your finger to make this charade convincing."

All the air left her lungs, leaving her feeling empty inside. "Do we have to?" A ring on her finger should feel special. This was wrong in so many ways and Jolie wanted none of it.

"The media will expect you to flash something at them and act the excited bride-to-be," Devin insisted.

Deep inside, Jolie wanted to kick the man for his callousness. Didn't he know how much this hurt her?

No. And she sure as hell wasn't going to tell him. A girl had her pride.

He looked up at her and held out the ring. "This was my grandmother's. I want you to wear it."

Now the tears really did well in her eyes and she blinked rapidly to keep them from spilling down her cheeks and ruining the Kendall ladies' hard work turning the frumpy office help into a modern day Pygmalion.

"Get up." She tugged on his sleeve. "I'll wear it, just get up." Jolie held her hand out and let him slide the ring onto her finger.

Once he slid the ring in place, Devin rose.

Jolie held her hand up to the light, pretending to admire the setting, when in fact she couldn't see through the wash of tears threatening to fall. Putting her game face on, she forced herself to smile while inside her heart broke into a thousand pieces.

Devin's hands circled her waist and pulled her to him.

God, he felt good pressed against her. If only it was for real.

He leaned down, his mouth hovering over hers. "You could at least look happy. You're grimacing." He pressed his lips to hers in a brief, chaste kiss, nothing like the previous one.

Stiff and uncharacteristically angry, Jolie clutched at the back of his neck, pulling him down to kiss her longer and harder, anger fueling her.

The attack backfired as heat melded them together. Jolie couldn't tell when the kiss turned from punishment to passion, only that when she came back up for air, the first limousine had left. "Our audience has gone, you don't have to fake it anymore." She pulled free of his arms and marched to the waiting vehicle.

The driver held the door for her and she slid in, careful to tuck the train of her skirt inside. It would serve Devin right if he tripped over it.

Jolie caught herself thinking bad thoughts and sighed. It wasn't Devin's fault they were stuck in this situation. If it was anyone's fault, it was hers for going to his condo the night before. None of this would be happening if she'd gone straight home.

Devin slid in beside her and the door closed.

For the next five minutes, Jolie sat in silence, staring down at the ring. It was everything she could have hoped for in an engagement ring. She preferred colored gems over diamonds, and the few diamonds surrounding the emerald only enhanced the stone's inner fire. "Your grandfather must have loved your grandmother very much."

"He did. From what I remember, he'd have done anything for her." Devin's voice was quiet, resonant in the back of the limo, the sound wrapping her in the intimacy of the moment. "Do you like it?"

Jolie nodded. "It's the most beautiful ring I've ever seen." Those darned tears pooled again. What was wrong with her? "Don't worry, I'll guard it with my life."

Devin lifted her right, ringless hand and held it to his lips. "I'm not worried about the ring. I trust you."

"With your business, but this is different." Jolie pulled at her hand, liking how it felt to have Devin's lips on her skin far too much for a boss/employee relationship. "This ring is a family heirloom, besides being worth a fortune."

"Relax." He continued to hold her hand, which had the opposite effect of relaxing her.

All she could think about was how he'd felt lying next to her…naked.

Jolie's skin heated and she fought to keep her breathing even.

"I missed you today," Devin admitted.

"What, couldn't you keep your schedule straight without me nagging?"

"I managed my schedule just fine." He frowned. "I canceled all my appointments."

Jolie laughed. "You can't run a business by avoiding it."

"I know, but I've been working on lists of possible

suspects for Ash to investigate. Including a list of people I've wronged over the past few years."

"And?"

"Now that I think about it, you should be top of that list."

"Why me?"

"I haven't told you how much I appreciate you. You keep me straight. Hell, you would probably make a better CEO than I do."

"It's part of the job."

"No, it's not. You put up with a lot of my crap and I just wanted to let you know that I notice. I think you're great."

"Nice to know I'm an appreciated executive assistant." If only he saw her as more than an executive assistant. She wanted to ask him, *What about last night?* Making love to him felt like it had been a dream from long ago. So much had happened since then. And Devin hadn't brought it up. Did that mean he wanted to forget it ever happened?

The brief respite from tension over, Jolie's nerves knotted anew. She was afraid if she mentioned their night of passion, Devin would admit he'd been a fool and it had been a disaster, not the magical experience Jolie would remember for the rest of her life.

The more she thought the more jittery she became. "I'm worried," she blurted out.

"Don't be. As we are the only ones in on this secret, the media will never know the difference."

"Not about the announcement of our engagement, but about Natalie." Her concern for her friend outweighed her half promise to keep the afternoon's incident to herself, and talking about Natalie might take her mind off a naked Devin.

Devin frowned. "What about Natalie?"

"She's limping because she was hit by a car today."

"What?" Devin's fingers tightened on her hand and he turned in his seat to face her. "Why didn't anyone tell me about this? Why isn't she in the hospital? Good God, did you see who did it?"

Jolie laughed and then sobered. "It's okay. She made me promise not to tell you and you can't tell her that I did." Jolie frowned at him. "Promise?"

Devin's eyes narrowed. "I'm not sure I can until I hear all the details."

Jolie told him about Natalie's concern that she'd been followed over the past few days and how she'd run out into the street to try to catch the man in the act. "So you see, it wasn't the cabbie's fault for hitting her. She's just lucky it was no more than a few bruises and sore muscles."

Devin started to speak.

Jolie held up a hand. "I had her checked out at the hospital, they took X-rays and all her bones are intact. She didn't hit her head and she'll live this time. Now can you promise not to tell her I told you?"

The worried expression never left his face and it grew more pronounced. "Why didn't she tell me?"

"Because she values her independence and you smother her," Jolie stated, her tone sharp and uncompromising. "Look, Devin, I know you want to protect her, but she'll keep pushing away unless you give her some space."

He faced forward, his gaze on the window between the driver's compartment and theirs. "I'm hiring a bodyguard."

"Great. She'll be ecstatic about that."

"And you won't tell her I told you that."

Jolie groaned. "Another secret? You don't pay me enough for all the subterfuge, Mr. Kendall."

"Miss Carson, are you considering blackmailing me?"

"Only if necessary." She crossed her arms beneath her breasts, her lips pressing together. "But one more secret and I'm walking. Do you hear me?"

He glared at her. "I can find another executive assistant."

"You can't even tie your own tie, how are you going to hire someone who can?" She shook her head and reached out to straighten the bow tie, slipping the knot free and retying it, not realizing until too late how close it brought them.

Devin captured her wrist as she drew away and pulled her closer.

Finding it useless to resist, she let him draw her into his arms.

"I like it when you get mad. Your eyes light up and little spots of color rise in your cheeks." He kissed first the right cheek, then the left.

"Careful, your sister and aunt spent hours on my makeup," she said, her voice breathy, hitching in her throat when he ducked to the side and slid his lips down the long line of her neck, across her collarbone to the swell of her half-exposed breasts. "You really shouldn't do that," she whispered.

"Why not? We're engaged." Devin raised his head, his lips hovering over hers, his hand cupping the back of her head.

"No, not really...."

Then he kissed her and all arguments flew out the window. Jolie lost herself in his arms, returning his kiss and more.

She didn't notice that the limo had come to a halt. Not until the door opened and bright lights blinded her did she consider the world outside Devin's arms.

Flashes blinked like strobe lights as dozens of cameras

snapped pictures of corporate giant Devin Kendall and his executive assistant kissing in the backseat of a limousine.

Devin got out first, shielding her from the cameras' harsh flashes. Once she stood and straightened her skirt, he moved her up beside him. He tucked her hand in the crook of his arm and smiled down at her.

Reporters descended, all asking questions at once.

The rest of the Kendall family had made it as far as the awning over the hotel entrance. Their crowd of reporters abandoned them for the latest arrivals, swarming around Devin and Jolie, giving them no room to move.

"Is it true you're dating your secretary, Mr. Kendall?"

"She's not my secretary," Devin responded.

"I'm an executive assistant," Jolie managed to grit out with her jaw clenched in a smile so fake she needed Vaseline on her teeth to keep her lips from sticking.

A female reporter shoved herself forward, a cameraman holding his camera on her, the light blinding Jolie. "Are there wedding bells in your future, Mr. Kendall?"

"We're here for the gala to raise money for a very worthy cause." Devin gave the reporter a direct look. "Could we please keep the focus on the St. Louis Children's Hospital?"

Devin wrapped a protective arm around Jolie and tried to edge his way through the throng. He hadn't made it two yards past the curb when another limousine slid to a stop behind them. Two valets opened a path through the reporters for the new arrival.

"Ah, as always the Kendall clan is well represented tonight." District Attorney Jesse Allen, dressed in a sleek black Armani tuxedo with a gorgeous young society debutante clinging to one arm, smiled expansively as the cameras turned briefly for a picture of the latest glamorous arrivals of the St. Louis elite.

Devin's hands fisted. The D.A.'s earlier inference to the potential of family being responsible for the Christmas Eve murders stuck in his craw. He nodded at the D.A. "Allen." He smiled at Jesse Allen's companion, whose micromini sequined dress stood out like garish costume jewelry among the gems of the night. "Lexi, does your daddy know who you're keeping company with?"

Alexis Rankin, only child of Margaret and George Rankin, old money of St. Louis, smiled petulantly. "Of course." She tossed her long straight bleached-blond extensions over her shoulder. "Daddy approves. He says it's always good to have a lawyer in the family."

"I see you brought your secretary with you tonight." The D.A.'s gaze rested on Jolie's cleavage. "Nice dress."

Jolie frowned. "My eyes are up here." She pointed at her eyes.

Lexi pouted and the D.A.'s face flushed a dull red.

Devin grinned at Jolie's straightforward attempt to put Jesse Allen in his place.

"Rather clever of you to deflect the media from the murder investigation by flaunting your paid lover." The D.A. tipped his head to the side, his eyebrows raised. "Isn't there another word for a paid lover?"

Jolie gasped.

Rage shot through Devin's veins and he took a step toward Jesse, his fists clenched and ready.

A hand hooked his elbow, holding him back. "Don't," Jolie said. "He's a little man with a little mind."

"I won't let him talk about you that way," Devin growled.

"Listen to her, Kendall. She's the only one with a lick of sense out of the lot of you. She's going after what she wants legally."

"That's it." Devin jerked free of Jolie's hand and would

have plowed his fist into the D.A.'s face if Ash hadn't stepped between them at the last moment.

"Jolie's right. He's not worth it." Ash laid his hands on Devin's chest and walked him backward, out of swinging range of the district attorney. "Come on, tonight is about the children, not us."

"Just let me hit him once," Devin muttered, low enough for Ash to hear, but not the media.

"You're causing a scene," Ash hissed in his ear. "Smile and remember who you are, like you always tell me." He spun Devin toward the entrance to the Four Seasons Hotel and gave him a push.

Devin shot a narrow-eyed glance over his shoulder at the D.A. "He can't get away with his insults."

"That's all they are and they make him look worse than you, unless you take a swing at him." Jolie rested her hand on his arm. "Now are you going to show your paid lover a good time, or shall we leave and give the tongues something else to wag about?" She smiled at him, the look playful and teasing.

How did she do it? How did Jolie take a bad situation and make it seem trivial? The tension in Devin's body eased. He had the most beautiful date of the evening and he wouldn't let anything Allen could say spoil the event for Jolie. She deserved so much better treatment than was being heaped on her and Devin refused to make it worse. "You are absolutely right. Let's give St. Louis something good to talk about."

"What about keeping our announcement low-key and discreet so the focus remains on the children?"

"I was wrong." Devin turned to the hovering reporters, who were anxious for anything to happen between Devin Kendall and the district attorney. "Excuse me, we *do* have an important announcement to make."

Reporters gathered closer, their camera crews blinding Devin with their floodlights.

Devin slipped his arm around Jolie and smiled for the camera. He leaned down to Jolie. "Do you want to tell them or should I?" he said, loud enough that most of the media personnel could hear.

Her pale face filled with a pretty pink flush. Instead of saying a word, she held up her left hand and flashed the emerald-and-diamond ring, forcing a smile to her trembling lips.

More than anything, Devin wanted to kiss those lips and make them tremble for an entirely different reason.

A combined "ah" went up from the mass of reporters and onlookers as the camera flashes exploded in their faces.

"Jolie and I are engaged to be married," Devin said.

"That's right," Jolie added. She leaned into Devin, her warmth spreading through the fabric of his jacket. "He popped the question today." She stared up into Devin's eyes as if she really was in love and was happy to be engaged to him.

For a moment his heart stopped and the world around him faded into the background. The only person he could see was Jolie Carson.

Then the reporters surged in, shoving microphones into his and Jolie's faces, bombarding them with questions.

Over the top of Jolie's head, Devin's gaze caught the district attorney's. Among the throng of well-wishers, one man stood out as less than pleased.

Jesse Allen stood on the edge of the melee, his eyes narrowed into thin, malicious slits.

Chapter Seven

"Care to dance?" Devin led Jolie toward the dance floor.

Her breath caught in her throat. She hadn't danced in years and to dance with Devin Kendall, the man she'd fantasized over...well, how much could a heart take in one night? She nodded and was swept into his arms for a heartbreakingly poignant waltz.

Despite his inability to tie his own bowtie, Devin Kendall was amazingly adept on the dance floor.

Jolie melted into his arms and let the music and Devin carry her away. For a moment she could forget the confusion of pretending to be pretending to be in love with Devin when in truth she'd been head over heels for so long, she couldn't remember when she hadn't loved him.

For a few short days, maybe weeks, she'd be free to act as besotted as she wanted...in public. In private, she had to maintain her cool, professional facade, lest Devin discover the truth. How pathetic would that be?

"You're thinking again." Devin's breath stirred the tendrils of hair loose around her ear. "What are you thinking about?"

You, me, us, making love. Jolie shook herself out of the stupor of her imagination. "Who did you have on your list of people who hate the Kendalls?"

"The two companies we acquired via hostile takeovers

and the employees we terminated over the past year. I checked over each and none seemed to jump out at me."

"A difficult task when you're the CEO. You weren't close enough to the trenches to see the impact on those people."

"And you were?"

Jolie smiled. "I'm an executive assistant. I can hang around the watercooler and listen to gossip when I need to. How did you think I heard about your marketing manager and the vice president of operations?"

Devin chuckled. "The watercooler?"

Jolie nodded. "Best communication network in the organization. News can travel both ways."

"So what you're telling me is that I should have had you make up the list?" His arms tightened around her and he spun her in a wide circle, smiling down at her as he did.

His smile and the twinkle in his eyes made her heart skip a beat and she almost tripped over her own train. In an attempt to keep the conversation light, she cocked an eyebrow at him. "I'm the best executive assistant there is. You said so yourself."

"Once again, you're right. I don't know what I'd do without you."

The lightness faded out of Jolie's steps. Devin Kendall would have to figure out how to live without her soon enough.

"Did you have Keith Cramer on your list?"

"Fired for sleeping on the job?" Devin nodded. "Yes. He got hired on as night manager at one of the big hotels around here. He's actually better off."

"How about Letty Morgan?" Jolie asked.

"I didn't have her on my list."

Jolie shook her head. "She had a druggy boyfriend who kept feeding her drugs. Remember her? I had you counsel her once. You tried to talk her into getting help, but she wouldn't. She ended up quitting."

"Why would she have something against Kendall Communication and the Kendalls if she quit on her own?"

"I'm not so much worried about her as her boyfriend. The punk wouldn't let her quit. She might have told him you fired her."

"I'll have Ash check him out."

The music ended and Jolie stood in the middle of the floor, Devin's arms around her.

"Where did you learn to dance?" she asked.

"My mother insisted at an early age. How about you?"

"My father taught me." Jolie sighed. "He was a good man."

"You know, you've worked for me for six years and I don't know anything about you. Where have you been?"

"Right beside you, your dedicated, invisible executive assistant."

Devin's gaze raked over her. "Not invisible anymore. I don't think I've seen a more beautiful executive assistant. How did you manage to hide this?" He waved his hand, taking her in from head to toe.

Heat rose in her cheeks. "I'm not beautiful. I'm dependable, efficient and effective. Just like your advertisement said six years ago. That's all you needed to know."

"Until now. Tell me more." He rested his hands on her hips as if it were the most natural thing in the world. "What about your father. Where is he now?"

Jolie's eyes misted. "He passed away while I was working my way through night school. My parents had me later in their lives."

"Your mother?"

"Died when I was twelve."

"So your dad raised you through your teens? That must have been a joy for him. I bet you were hell."

"Not really. My dad was great." Another song started up with a fast beat. "Shouldn't we move to the side? Unless you know how to swing?"

He grinned. "I do, as a matter of fact."

"You see? There's something I didn't know about you. I never knew you could dance."

"You know a lot more about me than I know about you." His hand slid up her bare arm, tracing the line of her throat and coming to rest at the back of her neck.

Her breathing quickened, her nerves jumping with the rise of his hand up over her naked back. "Like how you like your coffee with cinnamon in it and to stack papers on the right side of your desk, not the left. You like your shirts with medium, not heavy, starch and you prefer mustard over mayo. That about sums you up." She laughed, her voice shaky. "Everything I needed to know to survive the demanding Devin Kendall."

"I know something about you...." He leaned forward, his lips brushing her earlobe beside the white-gold earrings she wore.

Her breath hitched, her chest rising to rub against the front of his tuxedo, he stood so close. "Oh, yeah?"

"You like this." He caught her earlobe between his teeth and nipped gently, then he trailed kisses across her chin to her lips, where he hovered. "Am I right?"

She stared into his eyes, drowning in their blue depths. "Yes," Jolie breathed.

Devin kissed her, drawing her close as dancers crowded onto the dance floor. They stood in the middle, their feet still.

When Devin broke away, he ran a hand through his

hair and laughed. "I could use some air. Cold air. How about you?"

Her cheeks burning, Jolie nodded. "Definitely." A cold shower would be even better. Getting away from the source of heat would be the quickest solution.

As Devin led her off the dance floor, Ash was waiting.

"May I?" He held out his hands for Jolie. "I haven't welcomed the newest addition to our family properly."

Devin glared at his brother. "Bug off. She's tired."

"No, I'm not." Jolie smiled at Devin and walked into Ash's arms. "I could use a cool glass of champagne, though, after I've danced with your brother," she called out over her shoulder as Ash danced away with her.

As they spun around the dance floor, Jolie caught a glimpse of Devin, his brows angled low over his eyes, his face grim.

A smile tickled the corners of her lips. Take that, Devin Kendall. Maybe a little jealousy would do the man some good.

"He's as grouchy as a spring bear. You'd think I was stealing his bride." Ash grinned. "Don't worry. I have my own fiancée. And she suits me just fine."

"I'm glad to hear that."

"Besides, I can see from the look in your eyes, you've got it bad for my big brother."

Jolie stumbled. "You can tell?"

"Well, yeah. Everyone in the room can tell. Your face says it all. You're practically glowing with it."

Jolie lifted one hand to her cheek, heat rising. Could Devin tell that she really, truly loved him? Or would he think it just the act she was playing? God, she hoped he couldn't see through her. The man could read his opponents like open books, but she'd thought she'd done a pretty good job of hiding her feelings from him.

"So how long have you two been seeing each other that the rest of the family didn't know about it?"

"I've been working for Devin six years."

"No, not seeing each other in the office, but *seeing* each other. You know, intimately."

The heat consumed her and she looked away from Ash. "Not long." She hated lying to Ash or any of Devin's family.

"Devin must have finally woken up to what was right under his nose all this time. He's been so busy taking care of everyone else since our parents died, he hasn't had a life of his own."

"I suppose since he's the oldest of the siblings, he feels responsible for you all."

"He takes it a bit too much to heart." Ash spun Jolie around. "I think he felt responsible for our parents' deaths."

"How could he?"

"Natalie found them first. Devin found Natalie. Devin blamed himself for the murders, for Natalie's shock, for everything."

"Oh, dear. How old was he then? Sixteen?" Jolie shook her head. "What a horrible experience for a teen."

"Yeah. He kept saying that he should have been there for them." Ash shrugged. "I don't know what he could have done. The killer probably would have killed him, as well."

Jolie stared over Ash's shoulder at Devin. "No wonder he takes life so seriously. He's seen death."

"The good news is that he has you now. Do us all a favor and see if you can get him to lighten up on the rest of us, will ya?"

Jolie laughed. "I'll see what I can do." Like she'd be around much longer.

The song came to an end and Ash led her back to Devin. "I guess she'll have to do." Ash winked at Jolie, then kissed her cheek. "Welcome to the family."

A flood of warmth washed over Jolie. It had been a long time since she'd been a part of a family.

Natalie chose that moment to interrupt. "Come on, Jolie, I have to make a trip to the ladies' room and I don't want to go by myself." She grabbed Jolie's arm and dragged her away from Devin.

"So much for a walk in the moonlight," Devin muttered.

"I'll walk with you," Ash offered.

Devin faced his brother. "Not the same."

"She's a keeper, that Jolie."

Devin nodded, his gaze on the woman as she exited the ballroom. Yes, she was a keeper. Too bad the engagement wasn't for real. Any man would be lucky to have Jolie Carson as his wife.

"Once Uncle Craig hands over the check for our donation, we can leave, right?" Ash was saying.

"What's your hurry?"

"I can think of better things to do with my time." Ash's gaze migrated to the beauty in red talking with a group of men. Although petite, Rachel Stevens held her own—strong, intelligent, independent.

"What does she see in you?" Devin asked. "Does she know she's marrying a womanizer?"

"I gave up my black book and wild ways when I met Rachel." He shrugged. "Maybe she's marrying me because she's pregnant. I'll take her any way I can get her." Ash frowned. "Hey, I could ask the same. You're too serious and a workaholic. Why would Jolie want to marry you?"

Why indeed? If they weren't faking their engagement,

would a woman like Jolie be interested in a man like Devin Kendall?

Ash sighed beside him. "I don't know what our women see in us. I'm just glad they love us enough to look past our flaws and marry us, anyway."

Love. Ash was the lucky one. Rachel loved him and he loved Rachel.

Devin hadn't given love a thought since the day he'd found his parents' bodies. His remaining family and Kendall Communications had been his sole focus for so long he'd forgotten there was any kind of life outside that.

Jolie had changed that. Now he could barely focus on his family and the murder investigation. Especially with Jolie in the dress that showed so much of her assets....

From the corner of his eye, Uncle Craig caught his attention. He escorted Aunt Angela around the room as if she were fine porcelain to be carefully held and carried. He was attentive, loving and the perfect husband. "How does he do it?"

"Who?" Ash asked.

"Uncle Craig." Devin nodded to where his uncle and aunt stood in a group of cronies, laughing. "He makes being in love look easy. Hell, he's done it ever since I can remember."

"I think because he found 'the one' for him." Ash smiled and waved when their uncle looked up. "Unlike our parents. I was young when they died, but I can still remember the shouting matches they'd have. I never saw them hug or kiss and they never had a nice thing to say about the other. Why *did* they marry?"

"I don't know. But if they hadn't, us kids wouldn't be here today."

"You do have a point. And despite how bossy and demanding like an old mother hen you can be, I'm proud to call you brother."

"Same to you." Devin clapped a hand across Ash's back.

"Don't look now, but the D.A. is making a beeline for your fiancée."

Devin stiffened, his hand falling to his side.

Natalie and Jolie had emerged from a hallway and stood looking around the ballroom. Headed toward them was the district attorney, his date nowhere to be seen.

"What do you suppose he's up to?" Devin voiced his thoughts aloud.

"I don't know, but I don't trust him." Ash glanced at Devin. "Think we should cut in and save the girls?"

Devin frowned, remembering what Jolie had told him about Natalie guarding her independence. "No. They can handle it on their own."

"You're a better man than I am. I wouldn't let that lowlife, snake of a D.A. dance with my fiancée."

Natalie watched as the district attorney led Jolie to the dance floor. Much to Devin's chagrin, the band broke into a slow, sensuous tune.

His blood humming hot in his veins, Devin took a step forward.

Ash backhanded him in the belly. "Have you considered that Jolie might just be pumping our friend for information?"

No, he hadn't. All he could see was Jesse Allen's arm around Jolie. And the man's hand was far too low to be around her waist.

Devin's blood jumped from hot to boiling in seconds.

"Give her a minute," Ash urged. "What harm can he do during a three-minute song?"

The hand on her back moved lower to cup Jolie's bottom.

"Enough," Devin growled. "I'll kill him."

Jolie reached behind her back and pushed his hand up to the middle of her waist and kept dancing, a smile on her face.

"Seems your fiancée can handle the jerk. What else can you tell me about who has it in for us?"

It took a moment for Ash's question to sink in as Devin watched Allen's hand slide low again. "Who...oh, yes. Jolie recalled a young woman I'd counseled about her drug habit and her drug-pushing boyfriend. She quit after I'd urged her to seek help to get out of the situation."

"You think the boyfriend has it in for us?" Ash pulled a notepad from his inside pocket and a miniature pen from his trousers.

Devin glanced at his brother. "Are you always on the job?"

"Not always." Ash grinned at Rachel as she sailed toward him.

She grabbed his pen from him and tossed it over her shoulders. "Dance with me, or I'll find a man who will."

"Guess you'll have to manage on your own, bro." Ash followed Rachel out onto the dance floor, swinging her into his arms.

"Are you going to stand there and let that man dance with your fiancée?" Natalie stopped beside him, sipping on a glass of champagne.

Devin ignored his sister's taunt, biting down hard on his tongue to keep from grilling her. "How's that shopping leg?" he said, through gritted teeth.

The district attorney spun Jolie in his arms and dipped her low to the floor.

"Just a little sore. Nothing major," Natalie responded.

Devin stared down at his sister.

Her gaze shifted, a sure sign she was lying. Since their parents' deaths, Devin had practically raised his sister. He could read her like an open book.

Keeping Jolie's words in mind, Devin let his sister have her little lie. He'd take care of her in one way or another. He just wouldn't let her know. "You know I care about you, don't you, Natalie?"

"I know that." She glanced up at him, her eyes narrowing, her gaze searching his. "What brought that on?"

"Nothing. I just want you to know you can tell me anything. I'm always here for you when you want to talk."

"You're an engaged man. You're not going to have time to follow me around."

"I'll always have time for you." He slipped an arm around Natalie and hugged her, his gaze returning to the dance floor.

Anger surged through his veins when he noticed the D.A. had yet to pull Jolie out of the dip.

Jolie laughed, her breasts practically spilling from the top of her gown.

Devin leaned forward, ready to charge into the dancers and yank her out of Jesse's arms.

"She's gorgeous, isn't she?" A smile played at the corners of Natalie's lips. "You didn't see it until recently, did you?"

"See what?" His attention only half on his sister, Devin could barely contain himself.

"Jolie. I bet you didn't know what you had until the other night."

"I don't know what you're talking about." Devin hated to admit Natalie was right. He'd worked with the efficient, effective, bright and intelligent Ms. Carson for six years without actually seeing the gem he had. Now he couldn't take his eyes off her.

Natalie sighed. "I just think it's sweet."

"What?"

"That my big brother finally woke up."

The district attorney dragged Jolie back into his arms and leaned close enough to press his lips to her neck.

"That's it." Devin charged into the throng of dancers.

"Go get 'em, tiger," Natalie called out behind him.

The D.A. was in midspin, his hand resting on Jolie's rear, when Devin jerked him away from Jolie.

Jolie kept spinning, the train of her dress swinging around.

Jesse Allen's feet tangled in the train and he fell backward, landing in a decorative potted tree on the edge of the dance floor.

Laughter rose from those close enough to witness the scene.

The surprised look in the D.A.'s eyes struck a chord of memory in Devin, but he was too mad to analyze it since all he wanted was to plant his fist in the man's face. Devin stalked toward the man, but was pulled to a stop by a hand on his arm.

"Devin Kendall, what are you doing?" Jolie demanded.

He glared at the D.A., wanting more than ever to choke the snot out of the man.

Jolie's hand squeezed his arm. "Don't, please," she whispered, refusing to let go of him.

For a long moment, Devin struggled between his baser instincts and Jolie's voice of reason. Reason won out.

"We're leaving." He pointed a finger at the district attorney. "Stay away from my fiancée, do you hear me?"

"Just because you were born with a silver spoon in your mouth doesn't give you the right to push people around."

Jesse Allen pulled himself out of the pot and stood. "My father wasn't man enough to stand up to you Kendalls, but I am."

"I don't give a damn about your father, whoever he is." Devin's nostrils flared and he took a step forward. "I repeat—stay away from my fiancée."

"Or what, you'll kill me?" The D.A. dusted off his tuxedo, his face a mottled red. "Does murder run in the family?"

Chapter Eight

Jolie sat in her corner of the limousine, a good three feet away from Devin.

Whatever had come over him, he wasn't talking, and he scowled so fiercely he'd scare little children.

Was he regretting the engagement announcement?

"You know, we can use the argument with the D.A. tonight as an excuse to break off our engagement, if you'd like," she offered. "It would make sense." As soon as the words left her mouth, she held her breath.

"What?" He looked up as if he just realized she was in the vehicle with him.

Jolie took that blow to her ego, breathed and started again. "The fight at the gala. We could use it as a good excuse to break off the engagement. It's a perfect opportunity and we won't have to keep up the pretense."

"No." He scowled.

"Don't you at least want to discuss it?" she asked.

"No." He crossed his arms over his chest, his lips pressing into a very thin line.

"Well, then, I'll just sit in my little corner and keep my big mouth shut." She sat for a moment, bouncing her foot.

The scowl lifted for a moment. "You can't."

"Can't what?"

"Can't be quiet," he said.

"I beg your pardon?"

"Beg all you like. I at least know that about you." He snorted, his lips loosening into a hint of a smile. "You're busting to say something."

"I am not. I'm fine. I had a lovely time up to the moment you lost your mind and caused a huge scene."

The hint of a smile vanished. "He was feeling you up," Devin said tightly.

Jolie's lips twitched. "I had control of the situation."

"He was feeling you up."

"You're repeating yourself." Could it be the man was jealous? Jolie fought to keep from smiling.

"What were you thinking, dancing with that man? He only danced with you to make me mad. For some unfathomable reason he's got it in for the Kendalls."

"Thank you for that vote of confidence on my ability to attract other men, Mr. Kendall. It just so happens that I recognized his desire to irritate the Kendalls and that's exactly why I danced with him." She sat up straight, knowing full well it made her breasts jut forward. Nicely, if she said so herself, accented by the deep green of the dress.

Devin's gaze slid south of Jolie's eyes, his fingers tightening into fists.

Good. Let the man suffer just a little like she'd suffered for the past six years. "Allen was trying to charm me."

"Seduce would be more appropriate. No, grope." Devin leaned forward, as well. "You didn't have to put up with his sexual harassment."

"I was pumping him for information."

"Well, stop it."

Jolie's eyes narrowed and she refused to back down. "Devin Kendall, you're my boss. But let's get one thing straight…you employ me, you do not own me."

"We'd just announced our engagement. Doesn't that mean anything to you?"

"Our *fake* engagement. If it were real, it might be different." She sat back against the leather seat and looked away from him, pretending an indifference that just wasn't there.

She'd dreamed of being engaged to the boss, fantasized about a fairy-tale wedding on a beach in Tahiti and then cried herself to sleep at night when he never even saw her standing in front of his face.

"Well, for some damned reason, our engagement means something to me." Devin captured her hand, and pulled hard enough to yank her out of her seat and into his lap.

"Devin! What are you doing?" She struggled a moment, but he refused to let her go.

"Seeing you in Jesse Allen's arms made me crazy." He lifted his free hand and smoothed the hair out of her face.

Her breath caught in her chest and her struggles ceased, the warmth of his legs beneath her bottom burning through her gown. "Why now?" she whispered. "For the past six years I could have been a piece of office furniture for all the notice you gave me. Why now?"

"You're not furniture, Jolie Carson. I didn't see what was so obvious, so beautiful and completely compelling." He stared into her eyes. "I knew you were there. Hell, you manage my life. I couldn't function without you. But you're right, I didn't see you." His fingers trailed across her cheek, down her neck and lower, skimming the swells of her breast.

"You really are damaging my ego," Jolie whispered, closing her eyes, afraid to move, afraid the dream would end and she'd awaken, alone in her bed.

Devin released her wrist and cupped the back of her neck, twisting around so that she lay back against his arm.

His mouth descended on hers, capturing her gasp, taking her lips in a kiss so tender Jolie wanted to cry.

Neither noticed that the vehicle had rolled to a stop until the door opened and the chauffeur exclaimed, "Pardon me."

Jolie sat up with a jerk, tugging her gown securely over her breasts and smoothing a hand across her hair. She realized she still sat in Devin's lap and her cheeks flamed as she scooted across to exit the limousine.

She stood on the sidewalk looking around. They weren't at her apartment building. They were at Devin's condo. Devin unfolded from the limousine and thanked the driver.

"Wait," Jolie called out. "I need to go home."

"I'm going to take you in my car." Devin closed the door firmly.

"But why get your car out when the limousine is here? There's no reason for you to go out again tonight. The driver can take me home and you won't have to bother."

Devin leaned over and kissed her lips shut. "You're rambling, Jolie. You tend to do that when you're nervous." He kissed her again. "I'm getting an enormous amount of pleasure out of making you nervous. I *am* making you nervous, aren't I?"

Jolie's shoulders pushed back. "No, of course not. It's just been a long day. You need your rest and so do I." Hell, they hadn't slept much the night before. Her cheeks burned at the memory of lying naked beside him, remembered heat spreading throughout her body.

"Running?"

Jolie chewed her recently kissed lip. "Maybe."

"Have a drink with me, we'll discuss what happened tonight, then I'll take you home. I promise."

The chauffeur had already climbed back into the limousine, the door closing behind him.

What was Jolie afraid of? Certainly not Devin. Her lips still tingled from the kiss in the car and she'd almost forgotten that their engagement was one big farce.

Admittedly, Jolie was afraid of herself. She should be running screaming after the departing limousine. Instead, she let Devin cup her elbow in his strong, capable and utterly divine hand and lead her into the condo.

Nothing good would come of sleeping with Devin Kendall again. He'd wake up soon enough and wonder what the hell he was doing with the hired help. She wasn't one of the social elite. She ate peanut-butter-and-jelly sandwiches for lunch, not caviar. And she was in way over her head in this charade. The only person she was fooling was herself.

One fact loomed above all others in her mind—she would not emerge from this farce unscathed.

DEVIN UNLOCKED THE DOOR to his condo, stepped back and waved Jolie inside.

He tried to tell himself that he was doing Jolie an injustice. She'd only ever been good to him, taking care of him in more ways than was necessary for a good executive assistant.

When she'd asked him to let the limo take her home, he should have let her go. But he hadn't.

That dress, the way her hair swept to one side revealing the curve of her neck, and the swell of her breasts above the deep green neckline of her dress drew him in like a moth to flame. All he could think was how quickly he could get her out of the dress.

Not a good thought for the boss. The situation with Jolie went against everything he stood for. He'd crossed that line between boss and employee, violating one of the unwritten rules of leadership. How could he justify doing it again? He shrugged out of his coat and slung it over the back of a chair.

Jolie entered his kitchen and rummaged through the cabinets, opening and closing one after the other, her fingers moving nervously. "Damn it, where do you keep the coffee?" she asked, her voice shaking.

Devin had done that to her. Normally calm, cool and collected, his prize executive assistant was coming unglued. Because of him. Part of him liked that she was unraveling. That same wicked part wanted to unravel her even more.

With every intention of setting her back at ease, he stepped up behind her and caught her hand as she opened another cabinet door. "It's over here." He guided her hand to the next door, but he couldn't let go of her, or move away.

The scent of her perfume wrapped around him. The pale softness of her shoulders beckoned him like a siren calling a sailor. He couldn't resist.

His hand slid down from her wrist, over her forearm and lower, moving around to cup her breast.

She breathed in sharply, her body stiffening.

Had he overstepped his bounds? Hell, yeah. Could he stop now? Hell, no.

For a moment he hesitated.

When her body melted into his, he breathed for what felt like the first time in an eternity. He tugged her back against his chest, his desire pressing against her bottom, aching and needy.

He spun her in his arms and pulled her close, his fingers weaving through her hair, dislodging pins, loosening the tresses until they fell about both of her shoulders. "I like your hair down. You should always wear it that way."

All thoughts of being corporately correct flew out the window when Jolie's hands circled his waist and she held on tight, her hips pressing into his.

He kissed her, his lips slanting down over hers, his tongue driving into her mouth, thrusting and tasting, like a starving man on his first full-course meal.

He really should stop. It wasn't fair to her. He was the boss. She was his employee.

Jolie was a desirable woman and, based on her response to his kiss, she wanted him as badly as he wanted her.

Her hands dropped from his neck to slide between them, her fingers groping for buttons, slipping them free as fast as she could.

While Jolie worked her way downward to the buckle of his belt, Devin fumbled behind her, searching for the zipper that would free her from her dress. He tugged hard, but the gadget wouldn't budge.

Then Jolie had his belt undone and his own zipper slid like a knife through butter, his member springing free into the palm of her hand.

With fire burning in his veins, Devin could wait no longer. He bunched her skirts up around her waist, grabbed the backs of her thighs and lifted her onto the counter. He swept her panties down her legs and tossed them aside.

Jolie took him into her hand and guided him into her, her channel slick, wet and warm, her legs wrapping around his middle.

Devin thrust in, savoring how tight she was. He pulled halfway out only to be urged back in with her legs tightening around his back.

He held her hips steady as he moved in and out, the tension in his body building.

Jolie pushed his unbuttoned shirt from his shoulders, her hands sliding over his chest, pinching at his hard brown nipples.

Every touch sent jolts of electricity spinning through him, urging him faster, harder, deeper into her.

Her body tightened, her head tipped backward, her eyes closed, and she called out his name.

He wanted to please her, to make her as crazy and driven as he was, but he couldn't hold on any longer. He thrust one last time and then pulled free to keep from filling her with his seed. As deep as he was into heaven, he couldn't let himself get her pregnant. Not yet.

Jolie breathed hard, her dress still hiked up around her middle, her legs clinging to his waist.

Devin pulled her into his arms, resting his head on top of hers. For a long moment they remained entwined in each other's arms. Finally, Devin tipped her chin up and kissed the tip of her nose. "I promised we'd talk."

"Right." Jolie pulled him down to kiss her. "Talk."

He lifted her from the counter and carried her to his bedroom. There he set her on her feet, the fabric of her dress falling down around her to cover her long, sexy legs.

"You do realize we have a problem, don't you?" Jolie asked.

"Yes, we do." He nibbled at her neck, his hand sifting through her hair, letting it slide across his skin. He loved her long red, unruly hair. "You're wearing entirely too many clothes."

Jolie sighed, her hand cupping the back of his head as his kisses lowered to the rounded mounds of her breasts lifting up out of the bodice of her dress. "No, really, Devin. We have a problem."

He straightened. "We have several. Which one are you referring to?" With the tip of his finger, he angled her chin upward and pressed his lips to hers.

As Devin shifted his kisses to the line of her jaw, Jolie whispered, "We're breaking one of your own rules."

"Which one?"

"Fraternizing with your supervisor and staff."

"I can fix that." He trailed kisses down the side of her neck and across one bare shoulder.

"How?" She breathed in deeply, her breasts rising. "By changing the rules?"

"No, but I won't fire you."

She slapped at his chest. "Damn right. I'm the best executive assistant you've ever had."

"You're the only one I've ever had, as far as I'm concerned."

"No, really, Devin." She leaned her forehead against his chest. "The situation sets a bad example for the rest of the staff."

"I don't care. I'm the boss."

"Then let me make it easy for you. I quit."

His head jerked up. "Quit?"

She gave him a crooked smile that tore at his heart. "Quit."

"No, I won't let you." Jolie quit? Impossible. He wouldn't let her. "You signed a contract when you came to work for me that stated you'd give me two weeks' notice." Surely in two weeks he'd convince her to stay on. He had to. He needed her.

"Then consider my notice tendered."

"I refuse to let you quit."

"You can't stop me. And really, you shouldn't. It'll be for the best."

"The best for who?" He frowned down at her, his fingers digging into her arms.

"Kendall Communications and you."

Her talk of quitting had his chest so tight he could barely breathe. This situation had to change. Devin had to change Jolie's mind and fast. "What about Jolie Carson? Where do you fit in to the best for all?"

"Engaged or not, we've violated your fraternization policy. I see the only way to fix it is for me to quit. Problem solved. You'll no longer be fraternizing with your employee and we won't have to keep up the pretense of an engagement. No more lies."

"No. We've already dealt with that issue by announcing our engagement." Devin shook his head. "Besides, you are not sacrificing your career for my transgressions. None of this is your fault."

"Yeah, but the company can live without me. It can't live without you. And besides, it's too late. A verbal notice is just as binding as written. I'll have the written notice on your desk tomorrow. Now, will you take me home?"

He shook his head, utterly at a loss for words that could make her stay. He knew how stubborn she could be when she set her mind on something. "Did I do something wrong? Are you angry with me for something?"

"No. You did nothing wrong." She smiled up at him, and brushed back the lock of hair that had a bad habit of falling down over his forehead. "Well, besides breaking your rules and setting a bad example. But now that we've announced our so-called engagement, I can no longer work as your executive assistant."

He leaned close, cupping her cheek. "The last thing I want is for you to bear the brunt of my lack of control. I hate it when you make sense. But this time, Jolie, you've missed a key point. We've announced our engagement. It doesn't make sense to break it now." Devin reached out to draw her into his arms. He wanted to take up where they'd left off in the kitchen, but her body had stiffened and she'd withdrawn, if not physically then mentally.

Jolie's hands fell to her sides, no longer stroking his naked back as they had a moment before. "Take me home, Devin. Please."

Devin straightened, his gaze boring into her. Something had gotten to Jolie. The normally happy, efficient, capable assistant looked as if she'd just lost her will to live. "Stay here."

"No. I need time alone. Time to think about what I'm going to do after my two weeks are over. I have to put together a résumé, and hire a headhunter. Two weeks isn't much time when unemployment rates are as high as they are now."

"Your two weeks aren't over yet. And why do things have to change, anyway? Now that we're engaged, it will be okay. A few months down the road, when we break off the engagement, you can continue to work for me. We won't be fraternizing then."

"I'm not sure I can do this. It's not in my nature to lie." She stepped out of his arms and pushed past him, crossing the living room to the front door. "I'll call a taxi. No use you going out now."

"I'm taking you home, Jolie." His tone left no room to argue.

Jolie scrubbed her hands across her face as she waited by the door.

Devin gathered his shirt and buttoned his trousers, making note of the dark smudges beneath Jolie's eyes. Perhaps she was just tired. She hadn't gotten much sleep the night before and a lot had happened that day and evening.

That was it, she was tired.

Devin's step lightened as he led her to the parking garage located at the rear of the condominium. He settled her in the front seat and climbed behind the driver's wheel.

For a moment he sat with his fingers on the starter button. He wanted to say something to make it all right again, but the silence weighed heavily and he decided against it.

The drive to Jolie's modest apartment a couple miles south of his condominium stretched out in silence, the streetlights flicking by, casting light over her profile at regular intervals.

What was she thinking? Did she care whether or not she left Kendall Communications? More importantly, did she care that she'd be leaving him?

"Don't worry, I'll look for a replacement starting the first thing in the morning."

"I'll find the replacement, thank you," he snapped.

"She'll need training before I leave."

"You didn't have training when you came in."

She'd come in and taken over within a few days after landing the job. The only memory Devin had of life pre-Jolie was one of chaos in the office. How in hell did you replace someone who brought order to chaos?

He refused to think of it. Somehow he'd make her stay, even if he had to blackmail her.

The light over the front porch of Jolie's apartment wasn't shining as it had earlier that evening.

"That's odd. The light over the entrance is never turned off. The lightbulb must have burned out." Jolie unbuckled her seat belt slowly and opened her door before Devin could come all the way around the vehicle.

She gave him a brief smile. "Thank you for a lovely

evening. You don't have to walk me to the door. It's not at all necessary."

"I'm walking you to the door." He grabbed her arm and marched her toward the building.

"Okay, okay, at least slow down. Walking in heels takes a bit more finesse." She chuckled and slowed with him.

He matched her pace, his hand firmly on her elbow, refusing to let go, lest she made a dash for it.

Not that she would, but Devin was thinking crazy thoughts where Jolie was concerned. They entered the building and stopped in front of the elevator. The door slid open.

Jolie stepped in and turned to face him. "I can make it to my apartment by myself, you know."

"Hush." Devin stepped into the elevator with her. "You're sapping the chivalry right out of me."

She smiled up at him. "I rarely see that side of you."

"I'm fully capable of change."

"Not in the six years I've known you."

Devin didn't like the sound of that. But then he thought it through and came to the conclusion that as far as Jolie was concerned, she was absolutely right. He'd been so focused on business and family he hadn't bothered to look for areas of improvement in himself.

The elevator stopped on Jolie's floor and the doors slid open. Jolie stepped out first and laid her hand on Devin's chest. "I can make it on my own now."

Devin shook his head and hooked her elbow in his palm. "No can do. Not until I'm certain you're home and safe."

She turned and fumbled in her clutch for her key, and muttered, "Stubborn man."

"I heard that." His mouth twitched and he didn't bother hiding his smile. "I can be a very determined man."

"Hardheaded is the word." She stopped in front of her door and reached out with the key.

"You say potato, I say po—" His hand flashed out and stopped her from inserting the key. "Wait." Instinct told him something wasn't right.

"Why?"

Devin grabbed Jolie, swinging her to the side and behind him. Then, with his toe, he nudged the door.

Jolie gasped as it swung open.

Chapter Nine

Her heart in her throat, Jolie stepped around Devin. The slam of his arm across her middle brought her to an abrupt stop.

"Stay put." He pushed past her and entered her apartment.

She followed him regardless, her heart hammering against her ribs. Her place was a shambles. Furniture was overturned, the cushions of the couch were slashed, the stuffing spilling out on the floor. When she turned to face the wall over the couch, she gasped.

Boldly written in red spray paint across the wall were the words *Kendall's Whore*.

Jolie swallowed hard to keep bile from rising up her throat.

Devin cast a glance over his shoulder. "Call the police while I check the bedroom."

"No." She shook her head, her insides quivered and her knees threatened to fold. "We'll call the police from outside the apartment. If there is anyone still here…"

"I'll be fine." He tossed his cell phone to her.

"Wait till I call the police and let them check the apartment, Devin."

"It'll only take a minute." He smiled. "I'll be okay."

Jolie's hand shook as she held his cell phone. "Devin Kendall, today is not your day to die a hero."

He turned, grabbed her arms and kissed her full on the mouth. "Be right back."

Jolie held her breath as Devin disappeared through her bedroom door.

Two seconds passed like an eternity. She'd taken a step forward when Devin appeared again. "Empty."

Jolie let out the breath she'd been holding. "Thank God."

Devin took the cell phone from her nerveless fingers, pulled her into the curve of one arm and dialed 911. After reporting the break-in, he dialed his brother, explaining the situation. "Come on, we can't stay here, we might disturb evidence."

"But these are my things, my clothes. Everything I own."

"They're just things." He pulled her close, smoothing the hair from her face. "I'm just glad you weren't here when he broke in."

Jolie's body shook, a chill stealing over her that had nothing to do with the air temperature. He was right, she couldn't stay there. Her home had been violated. She'd never feel safe there again.

Devin removed his jacket and wrapped it around her shoulders. "We can wait in my car."

They descended in the elevator and exited the building. Devin's car stood at the curb where he'd left it. When they got close, Devin stopped abruptly and swore.

"What?" Jolie looked closer. All four tires had been slashed and someone had spray painted *Die! Die! Die!* all over the windows and doors in the same bright red paint they'd used on her apartment.

Devin pulled Jolie close and glanced around.

Jolie searched the shadows. Whoever had done this to her apartment and Devin's car had been there only a moment before.

"We can't wait here. Back in the building." He hurried her to the entrance and they waited inside, out of view from the parking lot until the police arrived.

The longer they stood there, the madder Jolie became. She pushed away from Devin and paced around the lobby. "Who would do such a thing? It's one thing to tear up my apartment, but your car…" She shook her head.

Devin leaned against a wall, his arms crossed over his chest. "To hell with my car and your apartment—those are just things. I'm more worried about you."

"I can take care of myself." She spun and paced back toward him. "Just let me get my hands on the jerk who did this."

Devin caught her wrists and held her in place. "You're not getting your hands on anyone. Leave it for the police."

"It just makes me so angry, I want to hit someone."

He balled one of her fists and raised it to his chin, a grin lifting the corners of his lips. "Hit me if it makes you feel better."

If anything happened to Devin… She stared into his blue eyes, the events of the past twenty-four hours bubbling up inside. Before she knew it, a tear slipped out, followed by another. "Damn." She used her free hand to swipe at the tears, only to give up when one turned into two, which then turned into a gusher.

Devin pulled her into his arms and held her. "It'll be okay. You'll see."

She sniffed loudly. "How do you know?" More tears slipped down her cheeks.

"I'll make it so." Devin dug in the front pocket of his jacket she still wore for the handkerchief, folded for show.

He popped it open and dabbed at her cheeks. "You're smearing your makeup."

"Your sister and aunt would be appalled."

"I don't know. I think they'd understand."

"They were so thoughtful and helpful. And here I am, a basket case."

"You're allowed. It's not every day a girl gets her picture on the front page, is forced into an engagement and has her apartment ransacked."

Jolie laughed, the sound ending on a hiccup, but the tears slowed and she took the handkerchief from him. "I'm sorry. I'm not usually so emotional." Though she liked where she was, she tried to push away from him. The more time she spent in his embrace only meant it would be that much harder to let go when she had to leave.

Devin wouldn't let her loose. His arms tightened. "Stay here. I like how you feel in my arms."

Despite her better judgment…oh, judgment be damned. She leaned into him, resting her head on his shoulder.

He felt so good, so right. If only…

Sirens wailed down the street, the sound increasing its intensity as the police neared her building.

Her pulse quickened and she pulled away from Devin.

They exited the building together and met Ash as he pulled his car into the lot.

"What happened? Are you two all right?" he asked, his attention going to Jolie's tearstained face.

"We're fine, but I can't say the same for Jolie's apartment."

"Or Devin's car." Jolie nodded toward the flattened tires and the spray paint.

Ash whistled. "Someone definitely has it in for you two. Let's get the reports written so that you can get out of here."

Devin and Jolie gave their report and watched from a distance as the investigators took pictures, dusted for fingerprints and made notes inside the apartment and around the damaged car.

The whole process took more than an hour. By the time they were free to leave, it had long since passed midnight. Jolie gathered a toothbrush and a few items of clothing that hadn't been damaged, then found Devin talking to Ash.

"Do you need a ride to your condo before I head for a hotel?" Jolie asked.

Devin nodded. "I do need a ride, but you're not staying in a hotel."

"I'm not?" Too tired to argue, she waited for his response, her body swaying with fatigue.

"You're staying with me," Devin announced. "Ash and I think it would be better if you weren't left alone."

Jolie sighed, too exhausted to fight.

Devin turned to Ash. "Family meeting in the morning?"

Ash nodded. "I'll be there as soon as I get through this paperwork. Looks like an all-nighter. You two be careful."

When Ash headed for his unmarked car, Devin turned to face Jolie. "You can't stay alone. Not until we find out who did this."

"No one shot at us or tried to stab me or you. It's just a break-in," she said as if break-ins were a common occurrence in her life. All she could think about was getting out of the dress and high heels before she fell. She didn't have a clue where she'd stay. Perhaps at one of the hotels nearby.

"You're exhausted. For once, let me take care of you." Devin slipped an arm around her, holding her steady.

"But—"

"No buts. We don't know what this person is capable of."

"I can stay with a friend," she protested, halfheartedly.

Devin frowned. "What friend?"

He had her stumped there. Jolie didn't want to bring any of her friends into the situation. It would be just one more person to lie to. But she couldn't stay with Devin, not when her resolve to maintain a safe distance was quickly melting away. "I don't know…a friend. How about Natalie?"

"You're staying with me. If it makes you feel better, you can have the guest bedroom."

It didn't make her feel better. Anywhere near Devin was trouble. Jolie couldn't keep her hands off the man. It was as if one night in his bed had unleashed a sexual beast she could no longer control.

"Where's your car?" He took her keys from her and let her lead him to the plain white sedan she used to commute to and from work every day.

Once settle inside, he headed for his condo.

Jolie's head lolled back on the headrest. "I'm sick about your car."

"Don't be. When I think what that bastard wrote on your wall…" His hands tightened on the steering wheel until his knuckles whitened.

Jolie stared across at him, noting how tightly his lips pressed together and the worry lines creasing his forehead. "They're just words."

"But you're not my whore."

"In a way I am." She smiled, though tears threatened to spill again. Who was this weepy woman? "We've slept together and you pay me."

"It's not like that. I didn't pay you to sleep with me."

No, she'd done it for free. What did that make her? Easy?

She closed her eyes to keep the tears from falling. She'd cried enough tonight. "I'm not as tough as you think I am."

"Oh, I think you're tough, all right. Tough enough to stand up to me and keep me on target. That's no easy task. This is all my fault."

She snorted. "How so?" She kept her eyes closed, enjoying the sound of his voice without having to keep up an appearance of being unaffected by the events of the evening.

"I shouldn't have…" His voice trailed off.

"Slept with your secretary?" She raised her head, challenging him to deny it.

"Executive assistant, and no. I can't regret that." His hand slid out to capture hers. "It's probably the most 'right' thing I've done in a long time." He sighed. "I shouldn't have gotten involved with you until we found my parents' murderer. All I did was make you a target along with the rest of the family." He squeezed her hand. "I don't regret getting involved. Just the timing. You're no longer safe."

"I told you, I can take care of myself."

"Yeah, I believe you." He squeezed her hand. "But I'm not letting you out of my sight until this is all over."

Warmth spread from where Devin held her hand throughout her body. It had been a long time since anyone had taken care of Jolie. She could get used to it, if she let herself. "Is that a threat, Mr. Kendall?"

"No, it's a promise. When this is all over, I'll make things right between us."

She opened her eyes and stared across at Devin. He was looking straight ahead, his expression tight, eyes narrowed.

What did that mean—make it right between them? Jolie didn't ask. She was afraid to. No scenario she could think of made it right between them. She didn't fit in the high-dollar, high-power world of the Kendalls. She wasn't all glitz and glamour. Jolie was…just Jolie, and she liked it that way.

As Devin approached the street leading to his condominium, Jolie took the opportunity to pull her fingers free of his grip so that he could turn, using both hands on the wheel.

Tomorrow…well, later that day, since it was already past midnight, she'd arrange for other lodgings. She couldn't stay with Devin. The more time she spent in close quarters, the harder it would be to leave him. And leaving was inevitable.

As they neared the condo, Jolie's heart beat faster. She still wore the dress from the gala. Returning to his condo only brought back memories of their lovemaking in the kitchen. How was she going to keep that from happening again? She had zero willpower to resist him.

Her breathing grew more rapid as Devin parked her car in the garage. She was out of the car before he could open it. The whole way up to his door, she tried to talk herself out of a panic attack. It was not like her at all to get this wound up over being with Devin. She worked with him on a daily basis. But that had all changed the night they'd made love for the first time.

As they stepped out of the elevator, Jolie stopped cold, a wash of desire flushing over her body, quickly followed by panic that she wouldn't be able to control her urge to touch Devin. "I can't do this. I think I need to find a hotel. Could I have my keys please?" She held out her hand.

Instead of giving her the keys, he took her hand and tugged her close. "Are you afraid of me?" He pulled her into his arms and tipped her face up to him.

As soon as his fingers touched hers she knew resistance

was futile. She couldn't avoid his eyes, couldn't lie to him. "No, I'm afraid of myself. Afraid I can't stop from doing this." She stood on her toes to kiss his lips, melting against him.

That single kiss unleashed a flood of desire so powerful she forgot everything, her panic transformed into a burst of passion. She dropped the clothes she'd been holding, her purse and sensible shoes.

Devin pushed his jacket from her shoulders as she unbuttoned his shirt. Then his hands stopped and he shook his head. "Not here." He bent and scooped her into his arms, his long strides eating the distance between the elevator and the door to his condo.

As he fumbled to hold her and remove his keys from his pocket, Jolie stopped kissing him and stared down at the floor.

"What?" He kissed her. "You're not getting cold feet, are you?"

She shook her head, her eyes narrowing. "Did you leave that box outside your door?"

His gaze darted to the box he hadn't seen in his rush to get Jolie alone. It sat next to his door, small, innocuous, covered in paper. Plain brown paper and sitting outside the door to his condominium.

"Don't you usually have all personal deliveries sent to the office?" Her arm tightened around his neck.

"Yes, I do. I'm never home to accept. This one doesn't have any markings on it." He set her on her feet and bent to examine the box. As he reached out, she caught his arm.

"Don't touch it." Jolie pulled him to his feet. "Do you hear that?"

He paused, willing his pulse to calm so that he could hear over the pounding of his heart.

"Ticking. Damn." He grabbed Jolie's hand. "Run!" Together they raced for the stairwell.

Devin reached it first and flung the door open, setting off the emergency exit alarm. "Go, go, go!" He pulled Jolie through the door. Just as the door closed, the world exploded.

Chapter Ten

Jolie's hand shook as she lifted her coffee cup to her lips. Her knees ached from where she'd crashed onto the concrete landing in the stairwell of Devin's condo, yet her lips quirked upward as she glanced across the office at Devin.

At least they were alive.

She was having a tough time keeping her mind on the conversation at hand. After the terrifying events of last night, Devin had asked his family to meet this morning. As tired as she was, it wouldn't take much for her to burst into tears.

"I'm glad you could all make it." Devin stood and paced, his steps measured, forceful, his expression serious. "The situation has escalated past dangerous to deadly." He pounded his fist into his palm. "None of us are safe until we catch the man responsible."

Jolie leaned her head back against her chair. Devin had insisted she attend this family meeting. Not that she didn't want to know what was going on, but she was on edge both emotionally and physically, having downed two cups of coffee already in an attempt to stay alert.

"My team is sifting through evidence as we speak." Ash ran a hand through his hair. He needed a shave and his eyes were as bloodshot as Devin's. "Whoever did this is leaving very little for us to go on. We canvassed the areas around both Jolie's apartment and Devin's condo, but there wasn't any other evidence. Most people were in bed asleep and didn't hear anything until the police arrived, sirens blaring, at Jolie's, or when the bomb exploded at Devin's."

"Not good enough. There has to be something." Devin glanced at Jolie's face. "We can't wait until one of us dies."

Jolie's hand went up to the cut on her cheekbone she'd gotten from falling into the stairwell. She was so thankful that the steel door had protected them from the explosion. Though the handmade bomb had not been that powerful, there was no telling how badly they would have been hurt had it gone off with them beside it.

Devin had a few bruises, too, having thrown himself on top of Jolie to protect her from the blast. As he stared across at Jolie, his hands tightened into fists. "I want everyone to travel in pairs, safety in numbers."

"You two were together last night as a pair, and it didn't help you." Natalie's brows rose, her expression challenging Devin. "I can't wait around for one of you to escort me everywhere I go. I refuse to succumb to this maniac's mind games."

Devin's mouth was set in grim lines. "He's passed the point of mind games and gone on to physical violence." He looked tired.

Jolie wished she could take all his worry away from him and shoulder it herself. She knew he felt responsible for his entire family, but how could he continue under the burden without crumpling?

"We can't run scared. We're Kendalls—it's not in us to be afraid and hide." Natalie planted her hands on her hips. "I'm not hiding." She held up a hand to stop her brother's next comment. "I'll be more vigilant and watch my back. I promise not to walk in shadows or stay out too late at night, but I can't put my life on hold for what 'might' happen. If I do, this guy wins."

Jolie smiled and said, "Amen, Natalie. I appreciate your impassioned speech and desire to maintain your independence at all costs, but Devin and I could have been killed last night. As it was, that bomb took out half of his condo. If we'd been a moment later leaving, we'd be lying in a hospital being pieced back together, or worse...."

"I get it." Natalie chewed on her lip. "I'm glad you two weren't hurt badly. But this is no way to live."

"Both women have a point," Ash said. "We can't be too careful. At the same time, we can't put our lives on hold."

"If I had my way, we'd pack up the family and leave for some remote compound where we can have a fully staffed security team enforcing the perimeter." Craig Kendall wrapped an arm around Angela's shoulders. "Everyone can stay at the family estate. I'm sure the security can be beefed up even more."

"Yes, there's plenty of room," Angela agreed.

Jolie held back a smile as Devin raised his hand.

"Jolie and I appreciated the hospitality last night and will continue to take you up on that offer until we can arrange for alternate accommodations. As for the rest of you, be careful and let us know where you're going and when you get there. Check in often. If we know where you're going, we know which direction to look if something should happen to you."

"Yeah, like being run off a road." Uncle Craig stood. "I'd hoped this was behind us twenty years ago. It was bad enough then. I hate to see it all happening again."

Devin's phone buzzed on his desk. His gaze shot to Jolie. "I thought I told you to have all calls roll over to the answering machine."

Jolie frowned. "I did." She rounded his desk and checked caller identification. The number indicated the front security desk at Kendall Communications.

"It's Security." She shrugged and answered on the next ring. "Devin Kendall's office."

"Ms. Carson, is that you?" Jolie recognized the voice as Steve, one of the guards who always said hello to her on her way in.

"Yes, Steve, what is it?"

"I was trying to get either Devin or Craig Kendall. It's an emergency."

"They're in a meeting, can I take a message?"

"Tell them the police are on their way up and they have a warrant for Mr. Kendall's arrest."

The world numbed around Jolie. "Which one?"

"I don't know. They just said they had business with the owners and flashed the warrant. They didn't give me time to read it. I had to let them through. I thought the Kendalls should know."

"You did the right thing, Steve. Thanks." With numb fingers, Jolie set the phone back in the cradle.

"What's happened?" Devin was beside her, pulling her into the curve of his arms.

"The police are on their way up with an arrest warrant for Mr. Kendall."

Angela gasped and leaned into her husband's arms.

"What's going on that we haven't heard about?" Natalie crossed the room to the television on the wall and switched it on. The St. Louis news channel had a special report airing. District Attorney Jesse Allen stood at the center of a crowd of reporters.

"God, I hate that man," Natalie said as she turned up the volume.

"—signed confession from the man who committed

the Christmas Eve murders. In his confession, he has implicated the man who paid him to commit the crimes as Kendall Communications owner, Craig Kendall. The confession and other evidence lead us to believe we've found the man behind the Christmas Eve murders."

"Damn." Devin turned to Ash. "Did you know about this?"

"No. I've been working on the apartment and condo attacks. No one at the station mentioned a suspect, warrant or confession."

Everyone in the room turned to Craig Kendall.

He stood, holding on to Angela's hand, his face white. He shook his head. "How can this be? I didn't pay anyone to kill my own brother. I loved him." He stared from Devin to Ash and then his gaze landed on Natalie. "You believe me, don't you?"

"Of course, Uncle Craig." Natalie went to her uncle and slid her arm around him, leaning her head on his arm.

At that moment, the door to the office burst open and Jesse Allen, surrounded by four of St. Louis Metropolitan Police Department's officers walked in. "Craig Kendall," one of the officers said, "you're under arrest for the murders of Joseph and Marie Kendall."

Before anyone could react, Angela Kendall sank to the floor.

Ash, Natalie and Jolie rushed forward to help. Devin clenched his fist, wanting to punch the D.A. in his smirk-ridden face.

Craig bent to help Angela to her feet. "Don't you worry, Angie. This is all a big mistake. You'll see."

"Runs in the family, doesn't it?" Jesse nodded at Devin's fist. "You look ready to commit murder."

Jolie reached out, caught Devin's arm and held on.

"That's right, hold on to him. You don't want us to make this a double arrest, now, do you?" The D.A. snorted.

Ash pushed his way past Jolie to get to Jesse.

Devin's arm clotheslined him. "Don't. We have enough to deal with without you getting suspended."

"Yeah, and lay one finger on me and I'll have your job." The D.A.'s brows rose in challenge.

Ash's eyes narrowed into slits. "I don't know what you're up to, but I guarantee I'm going to find out and take you down."

"I'm just here serving justice. That's all."

"Don't worry about me." Craig Kendall held up a hand, halting any further discussion. "This is all one big misunderstanding."

Devin moved forward. "We'll take care of Aunt Angela."

"I know you will." Craig turned to the police officers. "I'm ready." He held out his wrists.

The officer snapped a pair of handcuffs on Craig and led him toward the door.

"I'm calling our lawyer." Natalie punched the buttons on her cell phone and turned away to speak to the attorney they kept on retainer.

Uncle Craig glanced back. "I'll get it straightened out and be home in time for dinner." He smiled unconvincingly at his family.

"Don't count on it." Jesse Allen's lips turned up on the corners, his eyes narrowing as he smiled at Devin. "We have evidence that your uncle stood to gain a lot by killing his brother before you, his brother's oldest son, turned eighteen."

Uncle Craig stopped and turned, his face paling. He looked as though he might have a heart attack or stroke.

Jolie wanted to go to the man and help him.

"Your father didn't leave a will and, since all of his children were minors, the business went to his brother."

"My uncle owned half of Kendall Communications," Devin countered. "He helped found it and had every right to inherit the other half."

Jesse Allen wagged his finger back and forth. "No, not quite. You see, your uncle sold his shares to your father and started another business in California a few years before the murders. And what happened to that business?" The D.A. waited.

From behind Jesse, Devin's uncle responded in a dull, flat tone, "I'm not answering any more questions without my lawyer." Craig straightened, his jaw hardening. "Even if I stood to gain from my brother's death, it doesn't mean I had him killed."

"Sounds like a motive to me." The D.A. turned to leave. "I'll see you Kendalls in court."

"Oh, you'll see us and the best attorneys in the country," Ash said.

The district attorney laughed on his way out. The police officers escorting Craig followed, the group filling the elevator.

Angela shook her head. "I knew we'd lost money, but I didn't realize it had been that bad. Craig never told me."

"He probably didn't want to worry you." Devin hugged his aunt. "We know he's innocent. That's what matters."

"I loved you all like you were my own." She patted Devin's face, a tear slipping out of the corner of her eyes.

Jolie's chest swelled, her heart going out to the woman who'd taken care of the four Kendall children when their own parents had been murdered.

Devin escorted Angela as they followed the police officers to the elevator. Ash and Natalie trailed behind. As

Devin waited for the next elevator to take him downstairs, he looked back at Jolie. "Don't go anywhere. I'll be back as soon as possible."

Jolie could have laughed if she didn't feel so much like crying.

The elevator doors closed and Jolie was alone.

THREE HOURS LATER, DEVIN hurried back to his office, anxious to see Jolie. Natalie had taken Aunt Angela by her apartment earlier, promising to watch over her and see that she took a nap after all the trauma of the day.

The time he'd spent at the police station had proved fruitless. The detective in charge of the case had stated that Gene Williams, a man recently arrested for selling drugs, had voluntarily confessed to the murders of Joseph and Marie Kendall. He described the murder scene as it had been found by the investigators twenty years ago, noting details only those closest to the case would have been privy to. A very convincing confession.

Still, it was one man's word against another's as to who had hired Williams to do the job. But circumstantial evidence and the confession were too damning and had to be investigated. In the meantime, his uncle sat in a cell, waiting to be formally charged and for bail to be set. Guilty until proven innocent and stuck in jail until bail could be set.

The situation stank and nothing Devin, Ash or Craig could say would get Craig released from jail sooner than the next morning.

His chest tight with frustration and eyes burning from lack of sleep, Devin hurried the rest of the way to his suite of private offices.

His heart skipped several beats when he entered and Jolie wasn't sitting at her desk.

"I'm right here." She stepped up behind him. "I was in the ladies' room." She gave him a tired smile. "How're your aunt and uncle?"

"As well as to be expected considering Uncle Craig's been accused of murder." He stopped, closed his eyes and counted to ten, trying to get his anger under control. The more he tried, the less control he could muster until finally he shouted, "Damn it to hell!"

Jolie took him by the arm and led him into his office, pressed him into his chair and left him there without a word.

He counted to ten again, to no avail. Every nerve cell in his body was firing, making his skin crawl and his eye twitch.

Jolie appeared carrying a mug. "Here, drink this."

He grabbed the cup and downed a large swig, the next moment spewing the gulp across his desk. "What is this garbage?"

She crossed her arms over her chest. "Chamomile tea. Drink it."

"Where's my coffee?" he roared.

"You're not getting any. You're wound up so tight, caffeine will launch you into orbit." She pointed at the mug. "Now drink that tea."

Devin scowled at the woman. "Who's the boss here, anyway?"

"I quit in case you don't recall. I'm only here out of the goodness of my heart."

"Bull. You're here because you have a signed contract that requires two weeks' notice if you don't want to go to court."

"I could walk out that door right now, if I wanted."

"I'd sue."

Her green eyes sparkled, her lips twitching at the corners. "Sue me, baby."

He set the mug on the desk and lunged for Jolie, snagged her arm and yanked her toward him.

Jolie squealed and landed in his lap, nearly tipping them both over in the chair. "What are you doing?"

"I'm kissing my fiancée." He held her cheeks between his hands and kissed her. A long, slow, tender kiss. God, she tasted good.

Her arms wrapped around his neck and she settled against him, returning the kiss, her tongue seeking out his.

When they came up for air, he pressed his forehead to hers, all the weight of the past few days pressing in on him. "I don't know what to do."

"That's not like you." Jolie smoothed a lock of hair off his forehead. "You always have a plan."

"Not now. In all the scenarios I imagined, I never thought they'd accuse Uncle Craig."

"Just for the sake of argument, and not saying that he did, could Craig have killed your parents?"

Devin shook his head. "No. And it's not out of loyalty I say that. Uncle Craig doesn't have a mean bone in his body. Even in business. For as long as I've been CEO, I've played the heavy, making the tough decisions. He and Aunt Angela have been the best surrogate parents to us since my parents died. Hell, they were better parents than our own."

"After my conversation on the dance floor with the district attorney, I'd say he has an ax to grind with the Kendalls." Jolie stood and straightened her skirt. "Did you or Kendall Communications do anything to get him riled?"

Devin immediately missed the warmth of her against

him and would have pulled her back in his lap, but she moved out of reach. "I don't know of any connection we have to Jesse Allen." His eyes narrowed. "But I swear I've met him before. Not as the D.A. Maybe a younger version of him. He said something at the gala that I just blew off at the time."

"I seem to recall you were rather angry." Her lips curled in a smile. "You don't think as straight when you're angry."

Devin stared at his desktop, searching through the bits of his memory for just what Jesse Allen had said after he'd fallen into the potted plant. "He said something about his father not having had the guts to stand up to the Kendalls." Devin glanced up at Jolie.

"I'll call Ash and have him do a background check on Jesse Allen's father." She passed through the door of his office into hers.

"Before you do that," Devin called out, "get my brother Thad on the phone. With Uncle Craig in jail, he needs to be here."

"Dialing," she called out from the other room. "It's ringing. Pick up on line one."

Devin punched the button on his desk phone and lifted the receiver. As a photojournalist, Thad could be anywhere in the world. Their only way of contacting him was by cell phone. As the phone rang for the third time, Devin hoped Thad wasn't too far away. The family needed him.

On the fifth ring, Devin had shifted in his seat to set the phone in the cradle when a female voice answered, "Hello?"

Odd. Thad hadn't mentioned dating anyone; nor did he have time for relationships while gallivanting around the world shooting pictures of everything from wildlife to third-world civil-war carnage.

"I'm trying to reach Thaddeus Kendall."

"You have the right number. Thad's...not available right now. Can I take a message?"

Devin grinned. So Thad had a woman with him?

He hated leaving a message, but he had no other choice. "Tell Thad that his uncle Craig is in jail for murder and he needs to get home as soon as possible."

"Oh. Well. I'll let him know." The line went dead.

Jolie entered the office. "I told Ash to perform a background check on Jesse Allen's father. Did you speak with Thad already?"

Devin's brow furrowed. "No. I left a message." Devin didn't have time to think about Thad and his love life. "I need you to do a favor for me."

"Anything," she said.

A smile quirked the corners of Devin's mouth. "Anything?"

Jolie's cheeks reddened, her eyes lighting up.

"If my family wasn't falling apart around me, I'd take you into my arms and spend the rest of the afternoon exploring 'anything' with you," he said. "But I have to help keep the family together."

The color left her cheeks and she stared across at him. "You've always kept the family together. Let them help more. You can't always be the one to pick up the pieces."

"I have to." He leaned his elbows on the desk and buried his head in his hands. Exhaustion threatened to steal his determination, and having Jolie so close wasn't helping with his concentration.

"Why do you have to?" She rounded his desk and rested a hand on his shoulder.

He paused for a long moment. In the past twenty years

he hadn't talked to anyone about the night of the murders. "I owe it to my family. You see, it was all my fault my parents died."

Chapter Eleven

Jolie's mind reeled with Devin's words. "I'm confused."

Devin sighed and tried to let go of her hands, but she wouldn't release him. "My parents argued all the time. The night they were murdered they'd had a whopper of an argument. I couldn't take it anymore. I snuck out of the house and spent the night at my girlfriend's. When I got home, I found Natalie in my parents' room. She'd found the bodies first."

"And how does this make you responsible for their deaths?"

"Don't you see?" He gripped her hands so tightly it hurt, but Jolie held firm. "As the oldest, I should have been there," Devin continued. "I could have stopped it from happening. I most likely would have heard the intruder. Stopped him. My parents might not be dead now if I'd been at home. And what if the murderer had gone after my brothers or Natalie?" He shook his head, his gaze landing on where their hands joined. "I should have been there."

"Did you ever think that if you *had* been there, you might have been killed, too?" Jolie smoothed the hair back from Devin's forehead, aching for him and the amount of guilt he'd carried since he was little more than sixteen. "You can't blame yourself for your parents' deaths. You didn't kill them. Someone else did and he might have killed you, too, if you'd tried to stop him."

"But I was the oldest, and I wasn't there when I should have been." His voice cracked. "At the least, I should have been there to keep Natalie from finding them first. She was so shocked, she still has no memory of it."

"Which could be a blessing." The anguish in his impassioned words cut straight through Jolie's heart. In all the years she'd worked for Devin Kendall she'd known how committed he was to his family. But she would never have guessed that he carried such a huge burden of guilt.

"You are not your brothers' and sister's keeper. They're grown men and women now. They can look out for themselves. You've been so busy taking care of them, you haven't taken care of yourself."

Devin snorted. "They needed me. I wasn't there when my parents died, but I sure as hell will be there for them now."

"Sounds like you were probably there for them before your parents died. And your aunt Angela and uncle Craig were there, too. You didn't have to take it all on your own shoulders."

Devin shook his head. "You don't understand."

"Maybe not, but you have to start living for yourself."

"Not now. Not while Uncle Craig is incarcerated. God, I hate to think of what he's going through."

She laid a hand on his shoulder. "What about what you're going through?"

He pushed away from his desk and stood, shaking off her hand. "I'm not important."

Jolie took those words as a punch in the gut, feeling like she was unimportant to Devin, as well. "I see."

Devin stared across at her. "No, I don't think that you

do. I have to hold my family together. I'm the oldest. I can't let them down this time."

Jolie's chest tightened. He'd sacrifice everything for his family. That left little room for anyone else. Including her. "Is there anything you'd like me to do?" she asked.

"Ash's team at the SLPD is handling the murder investigation. In the meantime, we can't let our guard down until we know who is responsible for the most recent attacks."

"What do you intend to do?" Jolie could have guessed his answer.

"I can't sit around and do nothing. I need the address of the woman who was addicted to drugs and ended up quitting rather than get help. You mentioned she had a troubled boyfriend. He might have it in for our family."

"You can't go after him yourself. Let the police do it."

"I'll take Ash with me."

"Devin, please." She wanted to reach out, but he'd already shoved a deep wedge between them. Until the murder was solved and Devin's family was safe, he couldn't afford to worry about her. She had to accept that, whether she liked it or not. But he could get hurt chasing after the answers. "Please reconsider and let the police conduct their investigation."

Devin's expression hardened, his lips pressing into a thin line; his face could just as well have been set in stone. "My uncle is in jail for a crime I know he didn't commit. Maybe this isn't going to help Uncle Craig, but at least I'm not sitting around doing nothing. Maybe this woman's boyfriend had something to do with vandalizing your apartment, or the bomb at my condo. Jolie, I have to do something."

She had seen that determined look before and knew she couldn't dissuade him. "If you insist on going, let me go with you."

"No. Absolutely not."

Jolie squared her shoulders, fighting back the moisture pooling in her eyes. "If that will be all…" She didn't wait for his response, exiting his office without looking back.

Back at her desk, she pulled up the address for the ex-employee and jotted the information down on a piece of paper.

"Is my brother in?" Ash Kendall entered her office, his pace brisk, his jaw set and determined.

"Yes." She handed him the slip of paper. "Could you give this to him? It's the address of a former employee he thinks may be involved in the recent events."

"Good. I'll take it." Ash snatched the paper from her fingers and plowed into Devin's office.

Jolie had held it together as long as she could. With Devin occupied with his brother, she made a beeline for the ladies' room as the tears spilled over the edges of her eyelids and slipped down her cheeks. Thank goodness there weren't any other people to witness her losing it.

She shoved through the bathroom door and stood in front of the sink, willing the tears to dry and go away. Yet the longer she stood there, the more the tears fell until she was bent double, sobbing over the empty washbasin.

She didn't see the other woman until a hand reached out to pat her on the back. Through a film of tears, she recognized Angela Kendall's worried face.

"Jolie, honey, what's wrong?"

"Nothing." Jolie reached for a tissue on the counter in front of her and dabbed at the trail of mascara extending from her eyes to her chin. "Nothing at all. I'm fine." She forced a poor excuse for a smile, a sob rising up to ruin the effort. "What are you doing here? You should be with Natalie, resting."

"Oh, I'm stronger than anyone in this family gives

me credit for being. I wanted to speak with Devin and so Natalie drove me over. Please, Jolie, you can tell me what's really bothering you. I promise things will be better."

"How can they? My apartment is a disaster. Someone tried to blow Devin up. And your husband is in jail, accused of killing his brother and sister-in-law."

"Oh, honey. Yes, things are so crazy right now. But that doesn't change the fact that you're in love with my stubborn nephew." She lifted Jolie's chin and grabbed a fresh tissue, dabbing at the tears. "And, let me guess, he's so busy saving the world he's pushing you to the side?"

Jolie stopped crying and stared at the woman. "How did you know?"

"I know my nephew. He's got some misguided sense of responsibility for making his family happy so much so that he can't seem to make himself happy." Angela stood back. "There. Other than the bloodshot eyes, you look fine."

"But how will it ever be fine?" Jolie's tears erupted anew. "Good grief. I don't think I've cried this much since my father died."

"Love has a way of making fools of us." Angela smiled gently. "When I fell in love with Craig, I was a complete mess. I couldn't eat or think when I wasn't with him."

Jolie laughed and hiccuped. "Sounds like love isn't healthy."

"For some, it's not." Angela's smile faded. "Devin's parents fell in love in a whirlwind romance. But the longer they were married, the more out of love they fell. I suspect their marriage was on the rocks long before the murders. In fact, I truly believe Marie was having an affair."

"Devin mentioned his parents had a really big fight the night they were murdered."

"They were constantly arguing. Probably over Marie's

infidelity." Angela shook her head. "You'd think they'd have tried to get along for the sake of their children, but they were selfish and self-centered. I'd have given anything to have what they had."

"Their money?"

Angela's eyes glazed over with a sheen of moisture. "No, their children."

"Why didn't you have children of your own?" Jolie asked, her heart going out to the older woman.

"We did have a son."

"What happened?"

"He died in a car accident when he was only six years old." Angela stared down at her hands. "I'd been driving."

"I'm so sorry."

"Don't be, dear." Angela looked up at Jolie and smiled. "It was a long time ago and I've since had the pleasure of raising my dear niece and nephews." She smiled and patted Jolie's hand. "Don't worry, Jolie. Things will be fine, just you wait and see. The boys are going to clear Craig's name and have him back home in no time. And they'll catch the real killer and everything will return to normal. Then we can get on with planning your wedding. I so look forward to helping you."

Jolie rubbed at the knot of guilt building in her belly. This woman didn't deserve to be lied to. Jolie almost opened her mouth to tell Angela that she and Devin weren't getting married and that the whole engagement was a big fat lie. But she couldn't stand to see the look of disappointment in the older woman's eyes. Not right after her husband had been carted off to jail for a crime he didn't commit.

Angela hooked her arm through Jolie's and urged her toward the door. "Come. Since Natalie had work to do in her office, you can drive me home and we can talk about dresses and flowers to keep my mind off poor Craig."

No, Jolie didn't have the heart to tell the woman there would be no wedding or dress or flowers. She left the security of the ladies' room and walked back to the office to collect her purse.

Just as she was about to leave, Devin and Ash emerged from Devin's office.

"Ah, there you are. Natalie had called saying you'd insisted on coming here." Devin hugged his aunt. "We're headed out to Letty Morgan's place. Aunt Angela, do you mind staying here until we get back or until Natalie frees up from her work?"

"Don't you two worry about me. Jolie has offered to take me home. I'll be just fine." She shooed the men toward the elevator. "Go. Find something that will get Craig out of jail. The house isn't the same without him."

Devin lifted his aunt Angela's hands. "I'm not sure I like the idea of you out at the estate by yourself."

Angela squeezed her nephew's fingers. "I'll set the security system. Don't worry."

Still holding his aunt's hands, Devin stared across at Jolie. "Whoever ran Uncle Craig off the road the other day is still out there. So is whoever bombed my condo. We can't even be sure they are the same person."

"I'll keep an eye open for speeding cars and suspicious packages, and I'll text you when we get there and when I leave."

He opened his mouth to say something, then closed it and nodded. "Let's go." He headed for the elevator, Ash following.

"I really hope they find something." Angela's gaze followed the men until the elevator door closed between them.

"Me, too." Jolie gathered her purse. "Ready?"

"Yes. But I want to make one stop before we go home. I want to stop at the jail to make sure Craig is okay."

"We can do that." Jolie admired Angela. Though she was worried about her husband, she held it together for her family.

The trip across town, at the very beginning of rush hour, was mired in traffic. Jolie parked in the jail's visitor's parking lot.

"No need for you to go in. I'm not even certain they'll let me visit him. And I'm sure I'll be perfectly safe inside."

"I'll wait in the car, then. Take your time." Jolie wanted to think through all that had happened, and being alone was the only way to make that happen. She walked Angela to the front door and left her there.

As she turned to head back to her car, District Attorney Jesse Allen pulled into the lot and parked in a reserved space.

Jolie pretended she didn't see the man, wanting to avoid him at all costs.

"Ms. Carson, a moment please," the D.A. called out.

Pasting a fake smile on her face, she waited for him to join her on the sidewalk. If the man had it out for the Kendalls, Jolie might at least see if she could learn why.

"I wanted to apologize for last night and earlier today."

"What do you have to apologize for? I'd already forgotten," she lied.

Jesse Allen's lips thinned for a moment, then his easy smile, the one he used in front of the press, slid across his face. He lifted Jolie's hands and pressed a kiss to her fingers. "You are a lady. I don't know how you put up with Devin Kendall."

"Sometimes I don't, either." She twirled the ring on her finger.

"Tell me you aren't really going to marry that man?

What with his uncle in jail for murder and no telling what other crimes that family may have committed, you'd do well to rethink your engagement."

Anger burned through Jolie, heat rising up her throat into her cheeks. She forced herself to remain calm. "I don't know. Devin can be quite persuasive."

"Exactly. The man probably has a closet full of skeletons he hasn't told you about. But let me make it up to you for the humiliation of last night's drama."

Tamping down the urge to spit in the D.A.'s eye, Jolie asked, "How do you propose to make it up to me?"

"Join me for a cocktail party at my house tonight. I've invited all the elite of St. Louis. I promise you will see a much more cordial side to me and perhaps I can talk with you about your engagement."

Jolie ground her teeth, forcing herself not to reach out and slap the smarmy smile off the district attorney's face. The man clearly had issues with the Kendalls, and this was her chance to find out why. "Let me think about it. What time did you say your party was?"

"Seven this evening at my house." He drew a business card from his pocket. "Do you have a pen?"

Out of morbid curiosity and the budding beginning of a plan, Jolie handed him a pen and watched as the arrogant district attorney scribbled his home address on the card.

When he was finished, he handed the card to her, pressing it into her palm and holding on longer than was necessary.

Still smiling so hard her face hurt, Jolie tucked the card into her purse and waved. "Well, then, I'll be off. Perhaps I'll see you later."

"I'm counting on it." He made as if to reach out for her hand again.

Jolie turned and walked away as if she didn't see his

move toward her. If he touched her one more time, she'd either throw up on his shoes or slam her fist into his face. The man had no sense of courtesy or couth. But she had his home address. If Jesse Allen had anything to do with framing Craig for the murder of Joseph and Marie Kendall, perhaps she could find some evidence in the D.A.'s home.

"DO YOU THINK YOUR ex-employee hates you for firing her? Did she ever threaten you or the rest of the family?" Ash sat in the passenger seat of Devin's SUV as they drove across town.

"We didn't actually fire her. She quit before we could. The woman had been using drugs. We set her up with counseling, but she refused to go. It was only a matter of time before she was fired. You know we have a no-tolerance view on drugs."

"What about the boyfriend?"

"I think he was the reason she was having troubles. He showed up on occasion. Her supervisor had to have him physically removed from the building by security once."

"A real winner, I take it."

"Yeah." Devin tapped his fingers against the steering wheel as he drove through streets of St. Louis. "Ash, do you remember Mom and Dad?"

"I remember how much they argued. I was younger than you were when they died."

"Do you think most marriages end up like theirs?"

"Good God, I hope not. Why do you ask? Don't tell me you're already getting cold feet?"

How could Devin get cold feet when he wasn't really engaged? "No. I just wondered what makes a good marriage."

"I'm no expert. Maybe you should ask Aunt Angela

and Uncle Craig. They'd do practically anything for each other."

"Even commit murder?" The words came out before Devin could stop himself. He braked for a traffic light and turned toward his brother, trying to read his expression. Had he stepped over the line with his question?

Ash didn't answer right away, his focus on the road ahead. "Do you really think Uncle Craig killed our parents? His own brother?"

"No, no. Of course not." Devin shook his head, pressing down on the accelerator as the light turned green. "Although Craig had enough reasons to do it, a motivation that could convince a jury. He was broke, and he'd sold his shares of the company to Dad before moving to California. They'd lost their only child in a car accident. Angela wanted children really badly. It's enough to make a sane man do crazy things."

"Not Uncle Craig. He wouldn't do that. He doesn't have it in him." Ash laughed. "I can't even picture him with a gun or a knife in his hand."

Devin sighed. "I know what you mean. I'm not even sure why I brought it up. Sometimes I wonder if Mom and Dad killed each other. They were always at each other's throats."

"That would have been my first thought, but the evidence clearly indicated they were murdered in their sleep."

"What makes a couple fall apart like they did?"

"Getting married for all the wrong reasons in the first place. He was rich, she wanted to marry a rich man. I don't think they ever loved each other."

"I once overheard Aunt Angela and Uncle Craig talking about them. They thought Mom was unfaithful."

Ash glanced at Devin.

"Was this brought up to any of the investigators?"

Devin shrugged. "Not that I know of."

"That could be a key piece of data."

"I don't think Uncle Craig wanted Mom dragged through the papers after she died."

"Who cares? If she had a mystery lover, he could be the one who killed them."

Devin nodded. "Yeah."

"I'll check into it. That could put a whole different spin on this investigation. Mom had a lover?" Ash shook his head. "I never knew."

Several blocks went by before Devin spoke again as if the conversation was still going. "Which brings us back to the original question. What makes a good marriage work? Is love enough?"

"I think so. I'm marrying Rachel, aren't I?"

"But is it enough to keep a marriage together even after the lust wears off?"

"I believe a good marriage can be fun, but is like a garden that must be worked to maintain its health. You know, you reap what you sow."

From what Devin recalled of his parents, they hadn't done much toward maintaining their relationship. They had gone their separate ways for the most part. When they were together, they had never found common ground to stand on.

What would it be like to be married to a woman for a long time? Devin imagined being married to Jolie. If she was anything at home like she was at work, she'd always be a step ahead of him, never a dull moment, a challenge to his intellect. That was the upbeat, hard-charging side of Jolie.

The sexy, sensuous woman who shouted his name in the heat of passion was the other side of Jolie he hadn't known existed before the night she'd brought his dinner to the condo. Could he spend the rest of his life with one woman? A woman of multiple facets? A woman who would welcome him into her arms and challenge his mind?

Would he tire of her and wander on to a new lover every year? Devin shook his head. He couldn't imagine ever getting bored of Jolie. Not that he was marrying her. He couldn't give a relationship with her the proper care and maintenance it took to make a marriage survive. Not when he had family to look after.

"Here we are," Ash said.

Devin parked in the lot of an apartment building, his shiny new SUV standing out as too clean and well maintained to fit in among the clunkers lining the lot. A scrawny cat leaped from the trash bin in the back corner of the lot. Trash spilled out onto the ground, the bin overflowing with a week's worth of garbage.

As Devin shifted into Park, Ash opened his door. "You should stay in the car since you're not a member of the police department."

"You don't have backup," Devin reminded him, and got out.

"I don't like it," Ash continued as he rounded the front of the vehicle.

"I can take care of myself." He held up his hand. "Relax. You're the cop. Do your thing. I'll observe."

Ash sighed. "Fine. But I do all the talking."

"I can live with that."

They climbed the stairs to the second floor and walked along the balcony to the apartment number Jolie had written on the paper.

Ash knocked while Devin stood back a step, his gaze panning the parking lot below.

Footsteps sounded inside and someone swore. Then the

door opened and a bleary-eyed woman wearing a tattered bathrobe stuck her head out. "What?"

"Letty Morgan?"

"That's my daughter. What do you want with her?"

"We have a few questions for her." Ash flipped his wallet open, displaying his badge. "I'm with the St. Louis Metropolitan Police."

The woman frowned down at Ash's credentials. "What questions?"

"Is she home?" Ash asked.

"'Spectin' her soon."

"How soon?"

The woman lifted up on her toes and nodded toward a car entering the parking lot. "That might be her now."

Devin glanced at the car pulling in next to his SUV. A woman unfolded from the driver's seat. A young man with a hoodie, and the crotch of his jeans hanging down to his knees, got out of the other side.

"Excuse us, ma'am." Ash turned and hurried along the balcony the way they'd come.

Devin followed and then split off to descend a different set of stairs farther along the balcony. As yet, the couple hadn't spotted them.

Ash met the two at the bottom of the steps. Devin arrived at the bottom of his staircase at the same time. He ducked behind the metal stairs and waited just in case Letty recognized him.

"Letty Morgan?" Ash stepped in front of them.

The two stopped abruptly.

As soon as Ash flipped open his badge, the young man in the hoodie took off.

Devin braced himself as the man ran toward where he stood hidden behind the metal stairs. As he darted past, Devin stepped out in front of him.

The younger man shoved him hard with both hands and darted away.

Devin raced after him.

The younger man was fast but lacked endurance. He leaped over a bush, tripped and regained his footing.

Devin dodged the bush and kept running. The boy raced into an alley lined with fences on both sides. It didn't take long for Devin to catch up enough to snag the man's hood. He yanked hard enough to jerk him off his feet. He landed hard on the ground, rolled over and would have run again.

Breathing hard and ready to be done with it, Devin tackled him, landing hard on his legs.

Once he had a good hold on the younger man, Devin stood, bringing him up with his arm shoved up between his shoulder blades.

"Let me go." The younger man stood on his toes to ease the pain. "I ain't done nothin'."

Devin held tight, maneuvering him back toward the apartment complex. "Then why were you running?"

"You were chasing me."

"Not until you hit me."

"I didn't hit you. You jumped me."

Devin pushed the man through the bushes and out into the parking lot where Ash stood with Letty.

Ash stepped in front of the man. "I have a few questions for you."

"I ain't done nothin'."

Ash's lips twitched. "That's not what your girlfriend says. Where were you last night around eleven?"

"Watching TV with my girl."

"Oh, give it up, TJ." Letty shook her head. "They know you weren't with me."

"Only if you blabbed your mouth." He lunged toward her, but Devin kept him from reaching her.

Ash grabbed his free hand and held it up. Red paint clung to his dirty fingernails. "I bet if I did a comparison on paint, this pretty red fingernail polish will match the red paint on the car you sprayed last night." Ash dropped the man's arm. "You're already in deep trouble for breaking and entering and destruction of property. What I want to know is where you got the explosives to blow up the condo?"

The punk stopped struggling. "What explosives?" He shook his head. "I didn't blow up nothin'. You can't pin that on me. I didn't do it."

"Then you admit you trashed an apartment and spray painted a car?"

"Maybe." The punk looked from Ash to his girlfriend. "But I didn't blow nothin' up."

"Then who did?"

TJ shrugged. "I don't know, but it wasn't me."

"Why did you trash Ms. Carson's apartment?" Ash asked.

He jerked his shoulder, trying to loosen Devin's grip on his arm. "I don't know whose apartment it was."

Devin tightened his grip on the arm he held. "Then why trash the apartment and write the stuff you did on the wall?" He pushed the arm up higher.

TJ stood on his toes, his face creasing in pain. "Some dude paid me a hundred bucks to break in, trash it and write those words on the wall. But I didn't blow up no condo."

Devin loosened his hold, letting the boy drop down flat-footed. "What dude?"

"I don't know, he was wearing a cowboy hat down low over his eyes. He didn't give me no name, just gave me an address and paid me the one hundred dollars, telling me he'd see it if I didn't do it and he knew where to find me."

"Look, TJ didn't blow up anything." Letty laid her hand on Ash's arm. "He wouldn't know how. He spray painted that car and tore up that lady's apartment, but that's as far as it went."

"I'd have charged him more than one hundred dollars for blowing up a condo," TJ grumbled.

"Let me take over." Ash nudged Devin.

"No. If anyone is going to take the flack, let it be me. My boss can't fire me." Devin hiked the punk's arm up higher.

TJ stood on his toes again to compensate, crying out as he did. "Hey, I told you all I know, lighten up."

Ash pulled his cell phone from his pocket and dialed. "I'll have a squad car here in moments."

"You ain't hauling me in, are you? My parole lady is gonna have a fit."

"Should have thought of that before you broke the law again."

Thirty minutes later, Ash and Devin were on the road back to the office when a call came through on Ash's cell phone.

Ash hit the talk button and held the phone to his ear. "Kendall speaking."

Devin slowed as he entered the parking garage of the Kendall Communications building. He darted a glance at his brother.

Ash's face settled into grim lines.

Devin's pulse quickened.

"Yes, sir. Understood." Ash flung the phone on the floorboard. "Damn."

Devin brought the vehicle to a halt. "What was that about?"

Ash hit his palm on the dash. "Damn. Damn. Damn."

"That bad?"

"Yup." He stared straight ahead. "I've been pulled off the case as conflict of interest."

"You could expect that since you're Uncle Craig's nephew."

"Yeah, but that's not all."

"What else?"

"Gene Williams, the guy who signed the confession, escaped jail."

"He what?" Devin stared at his brother as the world crashed in around him.

"That isn't the worst part."

"What could be worse?"

"Someone ran him off the road, his vehicle flipped and he died before an ambulance could get there. So now they have a signed confession, the hit man is dead and the D.A.'s pointing his finger at the Kendalls, claiming we're trying to cover up the crime."

Chapter Twelve

Jolie braced herself when she heard the elevator doors open. She'd dropped Angela off at her house, making certain her security system was in place and activated. Then she'd hurried back to the office. She'd spent the rest of the day trying not to think of Devin.

Angela had it right. Being it love was messy. On the one hand she wanted to walk out the door and never come back. That would be the smart thing to do. Then she could get on with her life and start the grieving process.

Staying at Kendall Communications only prolonged her agony. She wanted Devin so badly she couldn't think. She'd been staring at the same email letter for the past hour and still hadn't read it.

When the elevator door pinged outside her office, her back straightened and she strove for a cool, calm appearance. Even if she was falling apart inside, Devin shouldn't be able to see it on the outside.

"No one saw the accident?" Devin was saying.

"No," Ash answered.

"Then how the hell can the district attorney point a finger at the Kendalls?" Devin blew through her office first, his strides angry, his fists clenched.

"What's wrong?" Jolie asked.

"What's right?" Devin shot back at her. "Get me Craig's

attorney, we're going to need more help in this. Hell, we might have to put his entire firm on retainer until this matter clears."

"I take it things didn't go well at the meeting with Letty Morgan?" Jolie paged through her online contacts list and located the attorney.

Devin faced Jolie. "No, that went fine. Her boyfriend admitted to trashing your apartment and my car."

Jolie glanced up from her contacts list. "What about your condo?"

Devin shrugged. "He claims he didn't plant the bomb."

Ash nodded. "We believe him. He's a small-time punk. Says someone paid him to trash your apartment and Devin's car. Whoever paid him knew enough to single out a guy with a plausible motive. Bet he didn't count on the punk's confession."

"Someone paid him?" Jolie looked up and blinked. Had she heard correctly?

"Yeah. And I'd bet my shares in Kendall Communications that same someone was responsible for bombing my condo."

Jolie sat back in her office chair, reminding herself to breathe. She and Devin could have been killed in that explosion.

"Someone has it in for the Kendalls." Ash turned to Jolie. "And that includes you since you two are engaged."

Devin leaned on the door frame of his office, his back to Ash and Jolie. "But the question is who? Who wants us dead?"

"I don't know." Ash turned toward the door. "But I'm headed to the station to get whatever information I can out of the detective they assigned to work the murder investigation. He owes me."

Ash left the office and silence reigned in his absence for a full minute.

During that moment, a thousand thoughts raced through Jolie's mind, one surfacing more clearly than any of the others. "I ran into the district attorney coming out of the county jail earlier."

Devin whipped around, his eyes narrowed. "What were you doing there?"

"Angela wanted to see Craig once more before she headed home."

"I don't like you running all over town when someone's trying to hurt everything Kendall."

Warmth spread through Jolie at Devin's words. He'd implied she was a Kendall. That little bit of joy was short-lived next to the giant problem they faced. "I was careful."

"What did he want?"

"He wants me to dump you for him." Jolie's lips turned up on the corners. "He's got a really high opinion of himself. Any reason he would dislike the Kendalls as much as he does? Have any run-ins with him?"

"Not that I recall. But his face reminds me of someone. I just can't quite put my finger on it. Someone from my past. Maybe in college or high school. I'm pretty sure I didn't go to school with a Jesse Allen. The name doesn't ring a bell."

"Maybe he's got a cousin you knew. Do you have year-books here?"

"Maybe. If they weren't in the condo when the explosion took place." Devin walked into his office and thumbed through the shelves completely covering one wall. "Here." He pulled out several books and carried them to his desk where he laid them out.

Jolie rounded the desk and stood behind him as he paged through the photographs of freshmen through senior students in his college yearbook. He started with the seniors and worked his way through the *A*s. None of the Allens that year fit Jesse Allen's bone structure and olive tones.

Devin shoved the book aside and opened the next one, thumbing through all the photos for his second year in college. Again, no one matched up.

"I could be wrong. He just might have one of those faces that everyone swears they know." Devin kept flipping through pages.

Jolie took one of the high school yearbooks, opened it on the corner of Devin's massive desk and started through the *A*s. As she passed the Allens she started to turn the page to a different class year when one picture struck her as familiar. She read the name. Jesse Alvarez.

"That's him." Devin stood so fast his chair toppled over behind him. He leaned over Jolie's shoulder, his eyes narrowed. "Jesse Alvarez...Alvarez... Why do I know that name?"

"Because you went to school with him?" Jolie offered.

"Yeah, but it's more than that. There's another reason." He lifted the phone off his desk and punched in several buttons, tapped the speaker button, then waited.

"Kendall speaking," a male voice said through the speaker.

"Ash, who do we know from our past with a last name of Alvarez?"

Jolie leaned forward, her hands clasped together to keep them from shaking. Had they discovered a clue? Was the district attorney somehow involved in sabotaging the Kendalls and setting up Craig Kendall as the fall guy for the murders of Joseph and Marie?

"Why do you ask?" Ash was saying.

"Because I can't remember." Devin leaned over the desk. "It's right there, but not coming to me."

"I can't think of anyone...no, wait. Didn't we have a groundskeeper by that name when I was a little kid? He worked for Mom and Dad, then Uncle Craig after the murder. First name was Juan or something like that."

"That's it. That's the one. Do a background check on Juan Alvarez and see where he is, if he had kids and where they are now."

"Care to tell me why?" Ash asked.

"I found a Jesse Alvarez in my high school yearbook who looks like a younger version of our district attorney Jesse Allen."

Ash whistled. "Coincidence?"

"Doubt it." Devin's gaze met Jolie's, sending shivers of awareness across her skin. "Check on it."

"Hey, one more thing, while I have you on the line."

"Yeah," Devin said.

"Scuttlebutt has it that the D.A. is on a Kendall witch hunt."

"And we're behind the curve on this one. Anything else?"

"Not so far. We have TJ Bryant in the interrogation room. He's not talking."

Devin swore. "Did the D.A. get to him?"

"That's what I've heard from one of my buddies."

"He might be the one who paid TJ to trash Jolie's apartment."

"They're not letting me near the kid." Ash sighed. "Everything I'm getting is second- and third-hand."

"Keep after it. Anything you hear, let me know immediately."

"I'll do what I can."

"That's all I'm asking." Devin clicked the off button

and stood staring at Jolie for a long moment. "Did the D.A. say anything else to you?"

"He invited me to his house for a cocktail party."

"Why?"

"I told you." She smiled. "He thinks I should dump you as a fiancé and take up with him."

"That would be a big coup for him. Seems he's been a very busy man over the past twenty-four hours. Jailed one Kendall, removed another from the murder case and is attempting to steal the other's future bride." Devin shook his head. "You're not going."

Jolie bristled. "Actually, I hadn't decided whether to go or not."

Devin's brows dipped deeper on his forehead. "You're not going."

"Is that an order?" Jolie's hands landed on her hips and she stood defiant in front of her boss and the man she loved. She'd be damned if he told her what to do on her own time, especially if it meant finding information that could help their case. "If Jesse has anything to do with framing Craig for the murder of your parents, don't you think it worth a visit to see if I can find evidence?"

"No. If he had anything to do with framing Uncle Craig for the murder of my parents' murderer, he's a dangerously angry man. Even if he didn't frame my uncle, he has a gripe against the Kendalls and he could be the one who tried to run Uncle Craig off the road and the one who blew up my condo."

"So? If he's invited me to a cocktail party for the St. Louis social elite at his place, he's not going to do anything idiotic with me there, especially if everyone under the sun knows I'm going there and anyone who's anyone will be there with me. He wouldn't be that stupid."

"Still." Devin crossed his arms over his chest. "I won't allow it."

Jolie's hackles rose along with her temper. "You do realize that what I do on my own time is my own business, right?"

"Not as long as you're engaged to me." A muscle in Devin's jaw twitched. A sure sign he was angry.

Well, tough. "Oh, please. We both know it's not a real engagement."

"As long as you wear my ring, it is."

Jolie's brows rose. "Is it?" She reached for the ring, preparing to pull it off her finger.

Devin held up a hand. "Okay, if you go to Jesse's tonight…I'll…I'll…fire you."

"You just do that, Mr. Kendall. I'm beginning to think I've wasted the last six years of my life working for you, anyway." She marched out of his office, grabbed her purse from her desk and headed for the elevator.

When she reached for the down button, a large hand caught her wrist and turned her around to face him. "I'm sorry. I was wrong."

Jolie's eyes widened, her breathing erratic, her heartbeat racing. "This has to be a first."

"First time I've admitted I was wrong?"

"No, the first time you've ever told me you're sorry."

"Well, I am. I shouldn't have ordered you to stay away from the D.A. I should have asked nicely." He pulled her closer, his arm sliding around her waist. "Please don't go to Jesse Allen's party."

"But I could look around for evidence he's involved in this case…involved, as in not in a good way…."

Devin kissed her, letting his lips touch softly against hers. "Please."

Who was she kidding? She couldn't resist the man when he was like this. "Well, when you put it that way…" Her arms slid up around his neck, dragging him closer, sealing their mouths together. Her tongue darted past his teeth, teasing and twisting against his.

The elevator bell rang behind Jolie and she jumped out of Devin's arms, straightening her skirt and hair. "You fight dirty, Mr. Kendall."

"That's Devin, Ms. Carson."

The elevator slid open and Natalie stepped through. She stared from Devin to Jolie and back. "I get the feeling I've interrupted something. I'll just head back down to my office…." She took a step backward.

Jolie reached out and grabbed her arm. "No, please, stay." Why she didn't let Natalie go, she didn't know. But suddenly she was afraid of being alone with Devin. Afraid she'd lose herself in him or make promises she couldn't keep.

"Yes, Nat, please stay." Devin pushed a hand through his hair and straightened his necktie. "I was just leaving."

Jolie's head whipped around. "Where are you going?"

"To talk with Uncle Craig." He touched a finger to the side of her cheek. "Stay safe, will ya?"

Jolie took his hand with hers and held it to her face. "Maybe I should go with you."

Devin bent to capture her lips again in a chaste kiss. "I'd prefer you stay here."

Natalie cleared her throat. "I'm still here. And having Jolie stay works out for me. I was thinking of getting something for dinner and needed a partner. Perhaps Jolie will join me?" Natalie turned a smile on her friend.

"I'm a bit hungry." Jolie gathered her scattered thoughts and nodded, her resolve strengthening. One that didn't include Devin or his permission.

As Devin stepped into the elevator, his eyes narrowed. Jolie had let him go too easily and, if he wasn't mistaken, that look in her eyes was one he'd seen before. The same look she had when she was cooking up something he might not like. As the elevator doors closed, he left her with a parting comment. "Don't do anything I wouldn't."

During the ride down in the elevator Devin wondered if he'd done the right thing leaving Jolie and Natalie alone. He rationalized that they'd be okay since he'd hired a bodyguard for Natalie. Wherever Natalie went, the bodyguard followed. He'd protect them both. As long as Jolie stayed with Natalie.

He made the trip across town quickly, dodging in and out of traffic to the St. Louis County Jail where his uncle had been locked up. On the way he called Ash and arranged to meet him there. If anyone knew what had happened to Juan Alvarez, it would be Uncle Craig. The background check Ash ordered would take time.

Ash was waiting inside, his lips pulled into a flat line.

"We've got more problems," he stated without preamble.

"What now?" Devin braced himself for more bad news.

"I've been placed on administrative leave."

"What? Why?"

"Until they determine who killed Gene Williams, the Kendalls are under scrutiny as the most likely suspects. That includes me. A freakin' suspect." Ash sucked in a deep breath and let it out slowly.

"You and I both know you didn't kill the informant. You were with me when we went to find TJ Bryant."

"They had an anonymous call that placed my sedan near the scene of the accident that ran Williams off the road."

"And they let an anonymous caller dictate your guilt?"

"Someone's wound tight at the police station. I did manage to pass the information about Juan Alvarez to a buddy of mine. He said he'd get back to me as soon as he had something."

"At least you have that. Looks like we're on our own to solve this."

"Yup." Ash removed his wallet from his back pocket and showed the supervisor, asking to speak to Craig Kendall.

Fifteen minutes later they were led back to a room where they could talk to their uncle.

Craig appeared older, the wrinkles around his eyes more pronounced. He still wore the same clothing he'd been arrested in. The trousers were wrinkled, the jacket missing, his sleeves rolled halfway up his arms. "It's good to see you boys."

Devin's heart twisted. This was the man who'd taken in all four of his brother's kids and raised them as his own. The man who'd been more of a father to them than their own dad. He had to free his uncle if it was the last thing he did. "Uncle Craig, what do you remember about Juan Alvarez?"

His uncle's brow furrowed. "Juan Alvarez? The name rings a bell, but I'm not placing him." He rubbed his forehead, the movement slow, his hand shaking.

"He was a groundskeeper for my father before the murders. Do you remember what happened to him?"

Uncle Craig looked up, his eyes widening. "Oh, yes, I let him go a couple years after I came to live with you."

"Why?"

"He wasn't doing the job we paid him to. He was lazy

and insolent. I'd warned him several times, but he didn't change, so I let him go."

"Do you remember whether or not he had kids?" Craig asked.

"As a matter of fact I do remember. When I counseled him about his poor work he begged me not to fire him, said he had a boy in college and he couldn't afford to keep him there without the job. But after a year of letting him slide, the estate was falling apart. I had to hire someone who would do the job."

"Possible motivation." Devin looked across at Ash. "Let's hope your buddy at the station has something on what happened to Juan."

"Let's go." Ash stood. "Uncle Craig, we're going to get you out of there as soon as we can."

"I'm not worried. Between you and my attorney, I'll be out soon. On bond, if nothing else." He waved his hands, shooing them toward the door. "Just go. I'll be fine."

Once outside, Ash pulled his phone from his pocket and dialed his friend at the station. After a few minutes, he had what he needed. An address for Juan Alvarez, right there in St. Louis.

Devin nodded toward his SUV. "I'll drive."

Ash grabbed a camera from the trunk of his vehicle and climbed into Devin's car.

Devin didn't have a problem with speeding and the sooner they got to the Alvarez house the sooner they'd have the information they needed about Jesse. His hands wrapped around the steering wheel like they would around the district attorney's throat if he had half a chance to choke a confession out of the dirtbag.

As he pulled out of the parking lot, his thoughts returned to Jolie. He wondered if she was still with Natalie and if the bodyguard was doing his job.

Chapter Thirteen

Jolie went to dinner with Natalie. She selected a bistro close to the Kendall Communications building, claiming she had more work to do when dinner was over.

As they entered the bistro, Natalie looked over her shoulder. "Do you see that?"

"What?" Jolie had been so sunk in her own thoughts and plans, she hadn't been vigilant about watching her back. Now she turned to look through the glass door to where Natalie pointed.

"That man standing on the corner. The one pretending to wait for a bus."

"Maybe he is waiting for a bus."

"Not when he followed us from the office to here. There are at least three bus stops between here and there."

"Think he's your stalker?" Jolie squinted, trying to get a good look at the man, but he was too far away to get a clear view.

"He's following us, but he's not the same man who'd been following me yesterday when I stepped out into the street."

"Please tell me you're not going to run out into traffic again." Jolie laid a gentle hand on Natalie's arm, prepared to grip tighter if the younger woman took it in her head to launch herself out the door after her stalker.

Natalie's lips pressed into a thin line. "No. I learned my lesson, but it doesn't make me feel any better. Do you think it's the same guy who tried to run Uncle Craig off the road and planted the bomb in front of Devin's condo?"

A chill ran the length of Jolie's spine. "Want me to call the police?" She had opened her purse to dig out her phone when Natalie's hand stopped her.

"No. I can take care of myself. I make sure I check both ways and behind me when I'm driving and I stay away from deserted streets. And if all else fails, I have my pepper spray." She patted her purse, her eyes narrow. "What I wouldn't give to spray him square in the eyes for following me."

"Hold on to that pepper spray until you really need it." Jolie claimed a table close to the window where they could keep an eye on the man across the street. She suspected the new "stalker" was in actuality the bodyguard Devin had told Jolie he'd hired to watch over his little sister.

The weight of all the lies and secrets was wearing on Jolie. She didn't have anyone she could confide in and she really needed to talk to someone about Devin and her crazy feelings for the man.

What she wanted was advice, the kind one got from a mother or best friend. But the fake engagement was a secret to the Kendalls, so that cut out Natalie as a confidante. Since she was Devin's sister, it wouldn't be fair to bring her into a conversation about her brother.

"What's eating you, Jolie? I mean besides being homeless, almost bombed and engaged to a workaholic." Natalie laughed. Then her face sobered and she laid her hand over Jolie's. "Really, what's wrong?"

"Nothing." Jolie ducked her chin, refusing to meet Natalie's direct gaze.

"For a couple engaged to be married, you two are as

jumpy as a pair of teens caught stealing kisses in the library." She squeezed Jolie's hand. "What's up between you two? Maybe I can help."

Jolie made the mistake of looking up into her friend's clear green gaze. "Oh, Natalie." Tears blurred Jolie's vision and she blinked to keep them from falling. One slipped out and dripped onto the napkin in her lap.

"Nothing's so bad we can't fix it. Come on, tell your best friend what's making the great Jolie Carson shed real tears."

Jolie laughed, hiccuped and let another tear slip down her cheek. She reached up to wipe it away and stared out the window without really seeing. "Promise not to tell anyone?"

Natalie crossed her finger over her chest. "Promise."

"My engagement to your brother is fake." As she said the last word, she turned to Natalie for her reaction.

Her eyes didn't bulge and she didn't gasp as Jolie expected. Instead she shrugged. "And?"

Caught off guard, Jolie leaned forward, her tears drying. "You knew?"

"I suspected as much, but knowing how much you love him, I kept hoping it would turn out for the best."

"Well, I'm glad I keep a secret so well." Jolie smiled and shook her head. "So, in your opinion what is the best? Engagement or not?"

"Engagement, of course." Natalie reached for her friend's hand again. "I've always wanted a sister and to have my best friend as a sister would be the best."

Jolie patted Natalie's hand. "I'd like nothing better than to call you sister. But that's no reason to be engaged."

"No, but the fact that you both love each other is."

"Love?" Jolie laughed. "Love doesn't work when it's only one-sided."

Natalie pounced on that. "Ha! But that's where you're wrong."

"No, really, it doesn't work when only one person loves the other." Jolie held up her hands. "Besides, Devin needs someone who can complement his station in life. And as much as I love all of you Kendalls, I don't fit in your world."

"What do you mean you don't fit? It's not as if we're space aliens or something."

"You're rich, you're powerful. You move in the highest social circles." Jolie raised her hands, palms upward. "I scratched my way through school just so that I could make a good executive assistant. I'm not a corporate giant. I can barely dress myself to go out for dinner. Heck, I'd rather wear tennis shoes and sweats than high heels and a dress."

Natalie sat back in her chair and crossed her arms over her chest. "Jolie Carson, if I didn't know you better, I'd swear you were a snob."

Jolie stared at her friend, aghast. "I am not."

"First of all, every one of the Kendalls works hard for what they have. They don't sit back on their laurels and live off their trust funds. Second of all, you're not simply an executive assistant. I've seen you in board meetings. You're just as knowledgeable about this company as my brother."

Jolie opened her mouth to disagree.

"Don't even try to deny it. My brother would be completely lost without you. He's smart, he's tough and he's in love with you." Natalie's lips formed a sad smile. "He just doesn't realize it because he's too busy being a big brother to the rest of us."

Butterflies swarmed in Jolie's stomach. Had Natalie

really said that Devin loved her? "He feels responsible for you all."

"I know. It's a blessing and a curse."

"Tell me about it." Jolie sighed. "When we announce the engagement is off, I'll be leaving Kendall Communications."

Natalie gasped this time. "Jolie, you can't."

"I have to. I've spent six years in love with Devin. I won't spend the rest of my life the pathetic executive assistant in love with a man who will never love me back. I deserve a life. I deserve love."

"Oh, honey. He loves you. Trust me." Natalie reached for Jolie's hand. "As soon as this mess is over he'll come to his senses. You'll see."

Jolie pulled her hand away. "I can't do it anymore. I can't be around him loving him like I do." In a softer voice she added, "And now that we've…been…together, I can't see him any other way. I can't work with him, knowing I'll never really have him. It's tearing me apart."

"It will be better soon," Natalie implored. "I promise."

"I don't think so. He loves you all too much to ever let go of his responsibility. And I wouldn't want him to make a choice between me and his family."

"You are one really mixed up lady, aren't you?" Natalie pulled a tissue from her purse and handed it to Jolie.

Jolie hadn't realized the tears had started again. She took the tissue and dabbed at her eyes, willing herself to buck up and get tough. She couldn't go to a cocktail party at Jesse Allen's with puffy eyes. The decision firm in her mind, she pushed her chair back and rose. "I have to go."

"Where?"

"I've been invited to a party I've decided that I really can't miss."

"You're going to a party? With all that's going on?"

"Believe me, if I didn't think it might help, I wouldn't." Jolie gathered her purse. "Will you be all right on your own?"

"I can take—"

"Care of yourself." Jolie laughed. "I know. But do be careful."

"I will." Natalie stood and hugged her friend. "Don't do anything crazy, will you? Let me talk to Devin. I bet I can get him to see what he's missing in you."

"No." Jolie's eyes widened. "You promised not to tell him about our conversation. He can't know that I spilled the beans on our engagement. And he can't know that I love him. It would be too...awkward, at least until I leave the company."

"Don't talk like that. I'll be bawling my eyes out before you get to the door."

Jolie smiled, though her heart hurt. "You'll be fine."

"Who will I go to lunch with? Who will I shop with?"

"I'll still be around, hopefully." Jolie hooked her purse on her arm. "Just not at Kendall Communications."

"It won't be the same."

"You're a Kendall, you'll survive." Jolie hugged her again and left before her eyes filled with tears and she changed her mind.

The sooner she found evidence that Jesse Allen was out to destroy the Kendalls, and that he was behind the attacks on Devin and Craig, the sooner they could call off the fake engagement.

She'd leave and finally get on with her life. Without Devin.

Tears threatened, lodging like a sock in her throat, but she refused to let them fall. She had to get back to her apartment, change into something more...seductive.... She hoped she could get around the crime-scene tape, retrieve her clothing and dress in time to be at Jesse Allen's by seven o'clock.

"THIS IS THE PLACE," Ash said as they pulled up to a house in a modest neighborhood on the south side of the city. This was the address for Juan Alvarez, father of one Jesse Alvarez.

"How are we going to handle this?" Devin asked. "You're not supposed to be on the case."

"Not to mention, being here will alert Jesse Allen that we're onto him." Ash sat for a moment. "I say we pull one from Thad's books. We go in as news reporters who've discovered a link between the Alvarezes and the Kendalls."

"Don't you think they'll recognize us as Kendalls?"

"No, just lose the coat and tie and mess up your hair."

Devin shrugged out of his suit coat and tossed his tie into the backseat.

Ash leaned across and ruffled Devin's hair. "There. Now you look like me." He grinned. "Scruffy."

"Whatever. Let's do this."

Ash handed his camera to Devin. "Let me do the talking. I'll be the reporter, you the photographer."

"Got it."

A four-door car sat in the driveway and the sound of a television blared through the walls of the house.

Ash rang the doorbell twice before the door finally opened.

Devin shuffled his feet, anxious to get on with this interview and back to the office. He had a bad feeling about leaving Jolie and Natalie. Although what could possibly happen with the two of them together in a crowded area of St. Louis?

The bodyguard hadn't called to check in or report on their movements, not that Devin had asked him to. Maybe he needed to have him report in at least every hour just so he could keep tabs on his sister.

Devin forced himself to take a deep breath and let it out slowly, pasting a smile on his face as the door opened and a man he could barely recognize peered out. "I'm not interested in buying nothing." He started to close the door, but Ash put his foot in the space.

"Sir, we're not here to sell anything. We're news reporters."

"Yeah, what do you want with me?" He didn't shut the door, but then he didn't open it wider, forcing them to talk through the crack.

"We received information that you used to work for the Kendalls of Kendall Communications back before the Christmas Eve murders."

"I don't know anything about the murders, I wasn't there when it happened."

"We're writing an exposé about the Kendall family then and now from the point of view of their friends, family and former employees. It will only take a few minutes. I promise. And it will be a big help to us to expose the Kendalls as the insensitive corporate giants they are."

Devin fought the growl rising in his throat. Ash was giving a convincing performance by bad-mouthing the Kendalls. So convincing, Devin wanted to punch him right in the mouth.

"Yeah, they are." Alvarez's eyes narrowed and he hesitated, then he opened the door wide. "Since you put it that way, come on in."

Devin didn't like lying to the man, but if Jesse Allen was behind what had been happening to his family lately, he'd be damned if he let it go any further, even if it meant telling a lie to the district attorney's father.

Ash settled on the sofa. "Mr. Alvarez, in what capacity did you work for Mr. Joseph Kendall?"

Devin sat beside Ash, his lips still, taking in his surroundings and the man who was Jesse Allen's father.

"I was the groundskeeper for five years at the Kendall estate," Juan said. "Until Craig Kendall fired me."

Ash nodded. "I'm sorry to hear that. Want to tell me what happened?"

"I was fine working for the other Kendall, Joseph. Worked there three years. Had a family to support. When Joseph and Marie were killed, Craig Kendall took a dislike to me and fired me."

"I'm sure that was a terrible loss."

"Sure was. When I lost my job, I couldn't make the payments on my house, so I lost that, too. My son had to help out with the bills and lost his scholarship. He had to quit college just to help out the family."

Devin leaned forward, ready to delve deeper into Juan's words.

Ash was ahead of him. "I'm sure you and your family suffered deeply for the loss."

"My boy had to put off college for years because of what Craig Kendall did. But Jesse showed them."

"How so?"

"My boy got his degree going to night school and then he went to law school." Juan Alvarez crossed his arms over his chest, a smirk curling his lip. "He'll make sure those Kendalls pay for what they did to us."

"Sounds like it, Mr. Alvarez." Ash closed his notebook and stood. "I think we have all we need, Mr. Alvarez, thank you for your time." Ash walked toward the door.

Devin followed.

"Hey," Mr. Alvarez called out.

Devin stiffened, feeling certain the old man had caught on to their little charade. He held his breath and turned toward Juan Alvarez. The older man spread his hands out wide. "Aren't you going to take my picture?"

Devin let out the breath he'd been holding, aimed the camera at the man and pressed the button. The man had nothing but contempt for the Kendalls. Well, the street went both ways. Juan Alvarez apparently didn't see why he'd been fired and probably never would.

As they stepped out into the open air, Devin breathed in a huge gulp of air and let it out.

Ash took the camera from Devin and slid into the passenger seat.

Devin stood for a few moments reining in his anger, then he slid into the sedan next to Ash. "It's Jesse Allen. He's behind this."

"We don't know that for sure. He's got the motivation, but we don't have physical evidence he was the one to run Uncle Craig off the road or that he set the bomb outside your condo door."

"You think his father suspected us as fakes?" Devin asked.

"Only if he knows anything about cameras. You took that picture with the lens cap on." Ash chuckled, his laughter building until it filled the car.

All the anger that had been building up during their interview with Juan Alvarez fizzled and his lips twitched. "I'll stick to running a corporation. You can be the detective."

"Deal."

They returned to the jailhouse, where Ash had parked his vehicle. Ash left for home while Devin hurried back to the office and Jolie.

Past normal business hours, he didn't expect to find anyone working except his executive assistant. Neither one of them had a home to go to. His would be under reconstruction for the next several weeks. Hers...well... she wouldn't feel comfortable going back to her apartment after it had been broken into.

They'd been so busy with everything that had happened, he hadn't thought far enough ahead to the night and sleeping under the same roof with Jolie at the Kendall estate.

His groin tightened and his strides lengthened, eating the distance to the elevator. The long ride up seemed twice as long. His pulse thrummed through his veins, the anticipation of seeing Jolie again new to him. How could she have worked for him for the past six years and he'd never really seen her? She'd quietly ordered his life, made it run smoothly and surprised the heck out of him when she'd climbed between the sheets with him.

Now he couldn't get enough of her. He wanted to spend every minute of his days with her, to touch her, taste her lips, feel her body next to his.

The elevator door slid slowly open. He pushed with his hand, eager to see Jolie.

As he stepped out into the hallway, he slowed his pace and took a deep breath, rounding the corner of the office door, ready to sweep the woman into his arms.

Her desk was empty.

Chapter Fourteen

Jolie pulled the edges of her long black coat around her as she stood on the porch at Jesse Allen's house. A glance through the windows at the guests milling about made her self-conscious of the simple black cocktail dress she'd worn for the party. She hoped it wasn't too casual, making her stand out when she wanted to blend in.

She patted her clutch purse, ensuring her pocket camera was indeed still there and stepped up to the doorway. A valet had whisked her car away to some unknown parking location nearby, putting Jolie on edge. If she wanted to leave quickly, she'd be slowed by the need to engage a valet to retrieve her car.

Her hands shook as she reached up to ring the doorbell. Before her finger connected with the button, a man dressed in a trim black suit pulled the door open and waved her inside.

She entered a spacious marble-tiled foyer. A monstrously large chandelier hung from the ceiling, the crystal facets sparkling. Elegantly dressed men and women spilled out of a room to the left of the entrance, where music from a four-piece ensemble played tastefully in the background.

Holy cow, how did a district attorney afford a place lik

this? Apparently Jesse Allen had more than made up for his modest beginnings.

The butler helped her out of her coat and directed her toward the sound of music and guests talking and laughing. "Please, the party is in there."

A woman carrying a fluted crystal glass of sparkling champagne stepped into the hallway laughing, the sound jarring Jolie out of her stunned perusal.

Jolie patted her hair and glanced at the butler. "Could you direct me to the powder room?"

"Down the hallway to the right, ma'am."

Jolie hurried in the direction the butler had indicated, feeling markedly out of her league in this grandiose house with its crème de la crème party guests. Why would Jesse Allen think she'd fit in with the upper-crust inhabitants of the St. Louis rich and famous? It had to be as she suspected, he wanted everything Kendall, including Devin Kendall's supposed fiancée.

If that was truly the case, then for tonight, Jolie had to pretend Jesse stood a chance of realizing his fantasy of stealing away Devin Kendall's future bride. She stood in front of the mirror, tucking the stray hairs into the pins holding her French twist in place. Her hands shook, reminding her that she was neither a smooth operator nor an undercover detective.

She was, however, an executive assistant to a corporate giant, privy to private conversations, serious boardroom wars and the secret of her engagement. If she could handle all that, she could handle faking an attraction to the district attorney. At least long enough to get inside the rest of his house and search for some evidence of Jesse setting up Craig Kendall to take the fall for the Christmas Eve murders. She also needed to find anything that pointed to the D.A.'s involvement in running Craig off the road or leaving the bomb at Devin's doorstep. Basically, she was looking for anything that looked as if the D.A. had a hand in everything that was going wrong in the Kendalls' world.

Jesse Allen was waiting in the foyer as she emerged from the hallway.

Jolie forced a happy smile to her lips and held out her hands, gliding into her role. "Jesse. It's so very good to see you again."

He took both of her hands in his and swept his gaze over her bare shoulders and down her torso.

His perusal felt like a lecherous hand creeping across her skin. Her cheeks hurt with the effort to maintain her smile when she'd rather slap the man's face.

"How did you manage to escape your fiancé to enter enemy territory?"

Laughing, she hooked her elbow through Jesse's and aimed him toward the throng of guests. "I told him I'd be at the mall shopping for sexy lingerie for our wedding night."

The D.A.'s nostrils flared, his smile widening. "I'd like to help you with that kind of shopping."

I'll just bet you would, you slimeball, Jolie thought, but kept her lips closed, the comment to herself.

Jesse continued, his arm circling her waist and drawing her close, "But I wouldn't be shopping for your wedding night with a Kendall."

"Oh, you don't think I should marry Devin?" She swatted at his arm playfully, pulling away a little. She couldn't seem too easy or the man would get suspicious. "I'm a grown woman, fully capable of making my own decisions. And Devin Kendall meets all the criteria on my list."

"Ah, a list, is it? I should have known an accomplished secretary like yourself would have a list."

I'm not a secretary, I'm an executive assistant, Jolie wanted to scream. Again, she smiled, her teeth grinding behind her lips.

"And what is top on your list of the 'right' attributes?" Jesse asked.

"Hmm…" Jolie tipped her head slightly. "It's a tie between bank account and clout." She smiled up at Jesse, batting her eyes, something she'd never in her life done until now. Playing make-believe wasn't quite as difficult as she'd originally expected. Especially with the right incentive.

Clear the Kendalls of suspicion.

In her mind, she repeated her mantra, making the slimy feel of Jesse's arm around her worth the trouble of not recoiling in disgust.

"Care to finish the dance we started the other night?" Jesse moved her toward the open floor space where several of the guests had already started dancing to the music provided by a string quartet tucked discreetly into a corner.

The district attorney pulled her into his arms, pressing the center of her back until her hips ground against his.

She couldn't mistake the hardened ridge behind his suit trousers for anything else. The man wanted her and she had to use that desire to her advantage. She needed information.

"With everything that's happened to the Kendalls in the past few days, why did you come here tonight?" Jesse said, his lips pressed to her temple.

Jolie paused a long moment before answering, appearing to consider her response. She'd already rehearsed the answer to this question on her way over to his house. "Perhaps because of all that has happened to the Kendalls in the past few days, I wanted to keep my options open. A girl never knows when she might be out of a job."

"Or an engagement?" Jesse laughed. "Reconsidering that, as well?"

She shrugged. "It depends on what other opportunities arise." Jolie pressed closer, rubbing against his erection, forming her lips into what she hoped was a suggestive smile.

Jesse pulled her yet closer, cupping her bottom with his hand. "Surely a pretty girl like you has plenty of opportunities available to her."

Jolie wanted to snort, but kept it from happening. Opportunities? She didn't even date. Her life had been centered on Devin Kendall for six years. How pathetic was that, considering they were engaged with no intent to marry? Still, she'd rather have a fake engagement with Devin Kendall than a pretend flirtation with Jesse Allen, any day.

Jolie had to focus on her role and her need for information. "I take it there is no love lost between you and the Kendall family?"

He leaned back and stared down in her eyes, his own narrowed slightly. "What makes you think that?"

Jolie gave him a sly smile. "I get the distinct impression that you're enjoying their fall from grace in the St. Louis social scene." She reached out and straightened his tie, letting her fingers climb up to his lips in an intimate assault. "I find it devilishly titillating."

"Titillating?" Jesse captured her hand and pressed his lips to the inside of her wrist. "I find you devilishly titillating, my dear."

"Enough to want to win me over from camp Kendall to camp Allen?" She stopped swaying to the music, her gaze pinning his, a sexy smile curling her lips.

Jesse Allen pulled in a deep breath and let it out slowly. "You're a very tempting woman, Jolie Carson." He glanced around at the crowd of guests. "Are you teasing me because you know that I can't do anything until all my guests leave?"

She widened her eyes in innocent appeal. "I'm sorry, did you think I was teasing?"

Jesse growled and gathered her close to his body.

Jolie fought not to gag over her come-on or his closeness. He didn't appeal to her at all; in fact, she found him revolting in his desire to steal her away from Devin. Still, she had to get him to believe she wanted him in order to win his tentative trust. "I believe your guests require your attention," she whispered into his ear, and nodded toward an advancing debutante who looked to have had one too many glasses of champagne.

To the debutante, Jesse Allen might have appeal. He wasn't bad looking and he did hold an influential position in St. Louis.

"It's your party. You should host." She stepped free of his embrace and smiled as the woman attached herself to Jesse.

Good. Maybe she'd keep him occupied while Jolie searched the house for evidence.

Jolie made a show of collecting a glass of champagne from one of the service staff and dancing away by herself to the opposite end of the room. Pretending to examine a painting, she watched for her chance to escape the living room and Jesse's watchful gaze.

Once she was in the hallway, Jolie wandered through the rooms on the main level of the two-story structure. Besides the main, open living area, there was a sitting room crowded with people either tired of standing or more interested in talking politics. Another door swung inward and outward with service personnel carrying trays of food and champagne from the kitchen.

The hallway that led to the powder room also led to a large closet and a guest bedroom.

Jolie assumed any evidence she might find would be in the study or master bedroom, neither of which were on the main level. She made her way to the sweeping staircase leading up from the foyer. She'd be seen by the staff and what guests were milling about the hallway and foyer. That couldn't be helped.

While Jesse was still in deep conversation with the debutante and a woman who appeared to be her mother, Jolie slipped up the stairs, making a quick pretense of studying the artwork lining the walls. As soon as she topped the rise, she ducked into the first room she came to. The moment her eyes adjusted to the darkness, she realized it was only a spare bedroom. She checked beneath the bed, in the dresser and closet for anything that could be construed as evidence.

When her search turned up empty, she quickly moved to the door and checked the landing before hurrying through the next door. The earthy scent of wood and paper struck her as soon as she entered the room. Darker than the first room, it took longer for Jolie's eyes to become accustomed to the limited lighting. She fumbled in her clutch for the LED flashlight pen she'd brought along for the occasion and clicked it on.

Bingo.

She'd landed in what appeared to be Jesse's home office or study. Polished shelves lined the walls filled with legal books and leather-bound classics. A massive mahogany desk graced the center of the room with a high-back leather office chair.

Jolie hurried to the desk, rifling through the unlocked

drawers, shuffling through papers and files of cases Jesse was working. Nothing jumped out and she was taking too much time. If she didn't get back to the party soon, Jesse would suspect she'd left or worse...he might come looking for her.

To be caught going through his personal belongings would not bode well for her or the Kendalls. If Jesse had stooped to running people off the road, setting bombs in condos and paying someone to trash her apartment, who knew what he'd do if he found her snooping through his house?

Jolie shivered, her hands shaking as she sifted through papers, searching for what, she didn't know. One drawer in the desk was locked. She removed a sharp letter opener from another drawer and jimmied the lock until it broke free. Figuring the letter opener might come in handy again, she slipped it into her clutch.

Inside the drawer was a yellowed picture of a family standing in front of a house. The back of the picture was dated twenty years earlier. The family consisted of a mother, father and a much younger version of Jesse Allen. Beneath the picture was a crinkled yellow letter from a local university. The letter stated a previously awarded scholarship given to Jesse Alvarez had been rescinded due to his inability to attend college that semester. The letter was dated two years after the Christmas Eve murders.

Jolie pulled her camera from her clutch and took a picture of the letter and the photograph, replaced them in the pile and dug deeper in the drawer.

She found another photograph of a young Jesse and a pretty young woman with strawberry-blond hair and green eyes. They wore sweatshirts with the name of the college Jesse had been attending written across the front. They looked the epitome of young, carefree college students, in love for the first time. The photo had been bent in several places and the edges were worn, as though it had been carried in a wallet or pocket for some time. She snapped a picture of the photo, as well.

As she reached the bottom of the stack of documents, Jolie had started to close the drawer when a bunch of envelopes shoved to the very back of the drawer caught Jolie's attention. Held together by a large rubber band, the top letter was postmarked six months after the letter rescinding the scholarship. The addresses were written in flowing cursive from Emma Schafer to Jesse Alvarez on each envelope.

Jolie pulled the first letter from the sheaf, opened the envelope, slipped the one-page letter out and unfolded it. Based on the wrinkles across the page, the letter had been wadded up at one time and then smoothed out. She shone her penlight down onto the words.

Dear Jesse,

I've missed you at school. I know that you and your family are going through a very trying time. I hope you will be able to return to school next fall as planned.

Since you've been gone, I've been busy helping out at the student center. It's given me a chance to meet a lot of new people and fill the time I would have spent with you, had you been here.

Your friendship has meant so much to me and I would never willingly hurt you. Which brings me to the part where I hurt you. I'm writing this letter to tell you that I won't be writing to you anymore. I've met someone new. He's majoring in marketing like me and we have so much in common. What I'm trying to say is that we're in love and he's asked me to marry him after we graduate. I said yes.

I'll always love you as a friend, but my fiancé gets jealous when I write to you. So this is goodbye. Know that you'll always be in my heart as a very dear friend.

Love,
Emma

Jolie's heart hurt for the young Jesse as she read the brush-off letter. He'd had a rough time of it having lost his scholarship and his girl all in the space of six months. Jolie snapped a picture of the letter, refolded it and replaced it with the rest of the letters where she'd found them at the back of the drawer. She eased the drawer closed and checked the desk over for any hidden drawers she might have missed.

Pictures of family, an old girlfriend and a letter revoking a scholarship weren't much to go on. If she hoped to find evidence of bomb-making materials, she wasn't going to find it in this office. Where would a man like Jesse keep stuff like that? Did he have a hobby room or workshop on the property?

Jolie left the office and moved on to the master bedroom in the next room, finding nothing but a closet full of the finest suits and sportswear, meticulously lined up, the hangers spaced at precise intervals. Moonlight shone through the open drapes pulled back from French doors leading out onto a balcony.

As she passed by the window, Jolie glanced out. To one side, but attached to the house, stood a building Jolie hadn't noticed when she'd driven into the circular driveway. It appeared to be a garage.

Jolie's pulse leaped. If the D.A. had driven Craig Kendall off the road, the car he'd used may be in that garage. A quick check through the rest of the rooms and closets on the upper floor left Jolie convinced she wouldn't find anything in the house proper.

Music continued to flow from the ballroom below as Jolie crept along the landing. She ducked low at the top of the staircase, hiding behind the railing as a group of guests moved toward the door followed by Jesse Allen.

Jesse smiled at the women, shook hands with the gentlemen and stepped out the door to send them on their way.

While Jesse stood with his back to the house, Jolie hurried down the stairs, schooling her face to calm should the man turn and spot her as she descended.

But his back remained to her as he waved at the guests pulling away in a shiny Jaguar.

Jolie followed a waiter to the kitchen, hoping the garage was in that general direction. She stopped to make a show of thanking the chef for the wonderful array of appetizers. Then while the staff reloaded trays for a return trip through the ballroom, Jolie sneaked out the kitchen door and across a breezeway to the five-car garage.

The door to the building was locked, but she didn't let that stop her. Figuring on the security system being down because of all the guests going in and out, she slipped the letter opener from her purse and went to work on the door lock. It proved to be harder to open than the desk, with a dead bolt lock that no amount of jimmying would release.

Jolie tucked the letter opener back into her purse, pulled a hairpin from her hair and tried again.

A door opened behind her, sending Jolie running for a nearby bush. The butler who'd been standing by at the front door to greet arriving guests had his jacket off and was headed for the garage. He pulled a ring of keys from his pocket and inserted one in the door. He entered, closing the door behind him.

Jolie, her heart in her throat, glanced left then right and ran for the door to the garage, hope soaring. When she tried the door, her hopes plummeted into her belly. The butler had locked the dead bolt behind himself.

The rumble of a motor and the mechanical clanking of gears announced the opening of an overhead door around the front of the garage. Jolie wondered if she dare sneak inside while the butler prepared to back a vehicle out of one of the stalls.

Careful not to be seen, Jolie rounded the corner of the garage and watched as an overhead door lifted upward. She leaned around the corner.

The butler was adjusting something on the dash, his attention on the control panel of the Mercedes four-door sedan he sat inside.

With her pulse pounding against her eardrums, Jolie slipped inside the garage and darted behind a mechanic's mobile tool cabinet. She waited for the butler to call out and tell her she was in the wrong place, but he didn't. Instead, he pulled the car out of the garage and stopped in the driveway outside.

A motor hummed above her head and the garage door descended between Jolie and the butler.

Alone at last, Jolie let out the breath that had been lodged in her throat. She stood, brushed the dust from her hands and hurried toward the three other cars housed in the garage. Each was covered with a soft cloth drape.

Jolie peeled the cover halfway off the first vehicle, revealing a bright red sports car convertible, top down. She replaced the cover and moved on to the next, recalling Devin mentioning that the car that had broadsided Craig's had been a dark, nondescript four-door sedan.

She hadn't noted any marks on the silver Mercedes the butler had removed from its bay and the paint was too light to be the one involved in Craig's attack.

She pulled the next cover up over a powder-blue antique Corvette. She'd seen pictures of these, but never been this close to one. Jolie didn't have time to admire its classic beauty as she moved on to the last car in the cavernous garage.

Her heart thumped in her chest as she reached for the cover and peeled it back. The dark sedan lying beneath was four-door just like Devin had said. Jolie hurried to the rear of the car, her breath catching when she lifted the dust cloth to reveal the lack of a license plate. Had she found it? Moving around to the right side of the vehicle, she held her breath. This was the side that would have collided with Craig's car, the side that would show the damage, if it had been the car to ram him off the road.

She lifted the covering, her heart plummeting to her knees. The paint job was unscratched, the fenders and doors immaculate and equally unmarred.

Her mission to find the evidence needed to prove Jesse Allen was setting up the Kendalls had been a bust.

Jolie let the cover fall down over the sedan, her shoulders sagging. When she looked up, she faced another door on the far side of the garage. Rather than exit through the door facing the kitchen, she'd be better off leaving through this one. Then she could circle back to the front of the house and ask a valet to retrieve her car.

Her footsteps echoed softly against the concrete as she neared the door. She twisted the knob only to find it had a lock on her side of the door. How odd. Why would the lock be on the inside…unless the door led to another room, not the exterior.

Retrieving the letter opener from her bag, she went to work on the lock, relieved to discover it wasn't a dead bolt. When the letter opener failed, she got out one of her credit cards and, like the thieves on television always did, she slipped her card between the door and the jamb and pulled the door handle toward her.

The door opened.

Too shocked to believe it, she stared for a moment, then rushed inside, closing the door behind her just as the overhead garage door opened again.

Her pulse pounded rapidly against the base of her throat as she stood frozen with her back to the door. Had whoever opened the garage door spotted her?

A car engine revved, the growl against the walls more noticeable than the actual sound, growing more apparent as someone moved a car into the garage. The overhead door rumbled to life again.

From all the vibrations, Jolie surmised someone had pulled the car back into the garage and closed it. Silence and stillness reigned, her breathing the only sound in the small room.

Jolie waited for two full minutes before she dared to think she might be alone again, and another minute passed before she allowed herself to move. Her eyes had done their best to adjust to the lack of illumination inside the room, but she could see very little. The room had no windows to let even the smallest amount of light inside and the door was sealed like a vacuum, no light filtering from beneath.

If no light filtered in, then none would filter out. She dared to click on her penlight, shining it around the interior of what appeared to be an office for the mechanic or chauffeur. Shelves lined the wall with tools, spare car parts, cleaners and wax. A desk took up one wall and a file cabinet the other. Partially hidden by the file cabinet was another door.

Ready to call it a night and realizing she wasn't cut out for the spy business, Jolie almost left at that point. But she was so drawn to the mystery door she couldn't leave until she discovered what was inside.

One more door and I'm out of here, she promised herself. Devin would be back at the office by now, maybe even wondering where she'd gone. They hadn't had time to discuss where they would sleep tonight, what with his condo bombed and hers a crime scene. Warmth crept over her body at the thought of coming up with a solution with her sexy boss. What could it hurt to have one more night with him? She'd quit the company as soon as the case was solved and Craig was released from jail.

The warmth chilled at the thought of leaving Kendall Communications…no, at the thought of never seeing Devin again. For years she'd been satisfied to love him from the background. Couldn't she continue on in the background?

No. Not after making love with him. It was time for her to move on.

Jolie squared her shoulders and crossed the room to the door. A metal latch with a padlock secured this door. How many locks did the man have?

No amount of coaxing with either the letter opener or a hairpin would open the lock. Frustrated and convinced the room could possibly hold the secrets that could clear the Kendalls, Jolie turned toward the room behind her, searching for anything that could help her get the lock open. Her gaze fell on a bolt cutter hanging against the wall. Allen would figure out someone was jimmying his locks soon enough—she might as well go for it.

Laying her clutch and the penlight on the desk, she hefted the bolt cutter from the wall and hooked it through the padlock's hasp. Using every bit of her strength, she bore down on the handles, thanking her fitness coach for all the bench presses. Just when she'd about given up, the hasp broke in two and the heavy metal fell to the floor with a loud clank.

Jolie froze and listened for movement outside the door. When no sound reached her ears, she leaned the cutters next to the door and removed the remaining hasp from the latch. She flipped the latch open and turned the knob.

The door opened on a set of stairs, leading down into a darkened room beneath the garage. Cool air wafted upward. Jolie grabbed her penlight and the letter opener and descended, chills raising gooseflesh on her arms.

Her light reflected off glass as rows and rows of wine racks came into view. So that was why he had the room locked. Some wines brought a steep price. He must have over a thousand bottles stored in the racks. No telling how much they were worth. But the wine wasn't evidence that Jesse Allen was sabotaging the Kendalls.

Jolie sighed. Another dead end. Disappointment almost had her turning back, but a light at the back of the wine cellar beckoned her to explore further.

As she cleared the last rack of wine, an overhead light-bulb glowed a dingy yellow over a makeshift work space containing a desk and shelves crowded with what looked like junk electronics and smaller hand tools. It was the photographs completely covering the walls that captured her attention. As she stepped closer, her breath caught and held. The photographs were of each of the Kendalls, and the one most prominently hanging over the desk was an eleven-by-fourteen picture of herself, stepping out of the Kendall Communications building.

Her heart skidded to a halt and she stood frozen.

"I wondered how long it would take you to find this room."

Jolie spun at the sound of the voice behind her. Blood raced through her veins, her heart beating so fast she thought it might explode from her chest. Her mouth opened to offer an excuse for being down there.

Jesse's hand rose before Jolie could get a word out. "Don't bother explaining. We both know you can't leave this room…alive."

Chapter Fifteen

Devin told himself not to get worried. As Jolie had told him countless times, she was a big girl completely capable of taking care of herself. Besides, what could possibly happen to her and Natalie when all they'd done was go out to dinner?

He checked his watch. Almost midnight was pushing it to still be out at dinner. For good measure, he searched for a note on Jolie's desk, anything telling him where she might otherwise be. No note, no message on his answering machine. Nothing.

Devin dialed Jolie's number. It rang five times and went to her answering machine. "This is Jolie, leave a message."

"Jolie, call me." Devin clicked the off button and fought to keep from throwing his cell phone against the wall.

Jolie always answered her cell phone when he called. Looking back, he realized how unreasonable it might be for his executive assistant to be on call 24-7, but he liked knowing she was only a phone call away, no matter where he was in the world.

His gut twisted as he thought of a hundred reasons Jolie wouldn't answer her phone. Each option was more dire and dangerous than the last. The last one he'd consider was that she was still having dinner with Natalie and they might just be enjoying themselves.

He speed-dialed Natalie.

"Hey, brother. Any news from Uncle Craig?"

"Where are you?"

"Nice to talk to you, too." She laughed. "I'm at my apartment."

"Alone?"

"If I had a man with me, I wouldn't tell you."

"No joking. Is Jolie with you?"

"No." Natalie's voice grew serious. "She left me at the bistro three hours ago. Where are you?"

Natalie's words sucked the air right out of Devin's lungs. "I'm at the office. Did she say where she might be going?"

"Yeah, something about a party invitation she couldn't miss."

Devin swore.

"What? What's wrong?" Natalie cried out. "Do you need me to meet you at the office? I can be there in five minutes."

"No, but do me a favor and call Ash. Tell him to meet me at Jesse Allen's house."

"Jesse Allen's? Was that Jolie's party invitation?"

"I don't have time to discuss it. Just stay put and wait to hear from me. Promise?"

"I'm not promising anything. If Jolie's in trouble, I want to help."

"Help by staying safe. I can't concentrate on Jolie if I'm worrying about you. Promise me."

"I'll stay safe," Natalie conceded reluctantly.

Not totally convinced, Devin didn't have time to argue. He had to get to Jesse Allen's place quickly. Three hours was a long time to be out of touch. "Gotta go, kid."

"Devin?" Natalie's voice stopped him from hitting the off button on his cell phone.

"What?" he asked, impatience making the word come out more harsh than he'd intended.

"She loves you."

"Who?"

"Jolie. You know that, don't you?"

Devin's heart swelled in his chest and then tightened. "Of course I know that. We're engaged, aren't we?"

"Whatever you say, brother. But she really truly loves you. Don't let her slip away."

"I have no intention of letting her go." Devin hit the off button and tried dialing Jolie again as he took off at a run toward the elevator.

He came to a grinding halt as he realized he didn't have a clue as to where Jesse Allen lived. Ordinarily he would have just asked Jolie to look it up. But her desk was vacant, and more than the desk, the entire suite of offices echoed with her absence.

Jolie made his world come alive, made him look forward to coming to work every day. She lit every room with her smile and intelligence, her dedication and beauty.

He refused to think of living a day without her. When all this was over he'd tell her how he felt.

His steps faltered as he entered the elevator. Just how did he feel about Jolie? Besides missing her when she wasn't around? His entire being ached to be with her. If it wasn't some serious disease he couldn't shake, then it had to be…no…he'd sworn never to let anyone or anything come between him and his family. He couldn't be…he'd refused to be…ah, hell, he was in love with a redheaded dynamo who'd risked her life to help him and his family.

As he slipped behind his car's steering wheel, his phone rang.

"Natalie called and gave me the message. You think Jolie went to Allen's party?"

"I know she did." Devin's teeth ground together. "Ash, I need Jesse Allen's address."

"I'm on my way there now, it'll take me twenty minutes to get across town." He gave Devin the address.

"I'm closer. I'll be there in ten."

"Don't go in until I get there. If I'm not mistaken, you aren't armed."

Devin hadn't considered a weapon. "I'll manage without one."

"Wait for backup, Devin. I'll call in the police, they'll handle it."

"If Jolie's in there, I can't wait around for the cops to show up."

Ash swore. "Don't be a hero, Devin. A dead hero is just that. Dead."

Devin tossed his phone into the seat beside him, punched the address into his GPS and blazed out of the garage like a man on fire. He gave the road his full attention, blasting through the streets, slowing only for the red lights and speeding through when the coast was clear. As buildings flashed by his mind went over and over what he'd learned that day.

Did Jesse Allen truly hate the Kendalls so much he'd kill to get back at them? Granted, if Jesse's father had lied to him about his reason for being fired he may think he had reason to hate the Kendalls.

But Devin found it hard to believe it was enough of a reason for a district attorney to want to inflict physical harm on someone, going so far as to risk his career in the name of revenge. But then Devin had seen even more successful men pursue revenge so fiercely they ended up losing their fortunes to their obsession.

And if Jesse had set out to hurt the Kendalls, Jolie was just one more weapon he could use in his pursuit. And she'd walked right into his trap.

His foot growing steadily heavier on the accelerator, Devin almost missed a turn, the GPS voice a heartbeat late in delivering the next direction.

Jerking the steering wheel hard to the left and jamming his foot on the brake, Devin set the car in a three-hundred-sixty-degree spin.

Tires squealed against pavement, trees whirled around in a blur and a gatehouse loomed in Devin's windshield before the car came to a stop, the engine dying.

His heart thundering in his chest, Devin forced himself to calm down. He'd be of no use to Jolie dead. He had to get there alive to help her should she be in a tight situation.

He switched the car back on and took off at a more sedate pace. The gated community in which Jesse lived had a wrought-iron gate with a keypad entry. The guardhouse stood empty.

To heck with that. Devin backed up, shifted into Low and slammed the gas pedal to the floor. He ducked as the car blew through the gate.

Iron bent and flew up into the windshield, cracking it and bouncing over the top of his car.

The GPS device led him through a maze of curves to the back of the subdivision where the houses sat on huge lots.

Jesse Allen's home stood at the end of the road. Devin cut his headlights and bumped up over the curb to stop behind a bush one-tenth of a mile from the structure. Lights shone from the porch, but the rest of the house stood in darkness. A lone car exited the driveway, headed back the way Devin had come.

If there had been a cocktail party, it had broken up long

before Devin arrived. The car that passed was a beat-up clunker, probably belonging to one of the catering staff.

Devin climbed out of the car and walked along the edge of the street, hugging the shadows until he arrived at the house. His first inclination was to barge through the front door and demand to know where Jolie was.

Instead, he circled the house, wondering if she was all right. She had to have come to Jesse's hoping to help. It was in her nature. It was one of the many traits he valued in Jolie. And she had so many great qualities he was only just beginning to appreciate.

Devin eased up to the window closest to him. He could see movement inside. The caterers' helpers were cleaning up. From one window to the next he moved, feeling like a Peeping Tom, but not caring. He had to find Jolie, and his gut told him to find her sooner than later.

When he realized she wasn't on the first level, he rounded the house to the formal garden in the rear and located a French door that had been left unlocked. His pulse hammered through his veins as he slipped inside.

A member of the catering staff chose that moment to duck into the room.

Devin hid behind the drapes, sure his shoes were sticking out, but he could do little else.

A voice called out from the hallway, "Mr. Allen said not to worry about this room. He wants us out in five minutes. We can return in the morning for cleanup."

Footsteps retreated and the room fell into silence.

Devin stepped from behind the curtains and ran for the door leading into the rest of the house. Waitstaff hurriedly gathered what little trash was in their way and headed for a single swinging door that led to a kitchen, talking quietly as they passed through. Soon the lower floor emptied of people.

Devin moved from room to room, already certain in his mind that he wouldn't find Jolie in any of these. He checked every door, every closet, thinking how futile the effort until he stumbled across a large hall closet empty but for one long black coat. A woman's coat. He fingered the fabric and brought it to his nose.

The scent immediately brought images of Jolie sliding into the limo next to him on their way to the gala he'd taken her to just last night.

His heart sank into his shoes. She'd been here. Might still be here, based on the coat hanging in the closet. He left it there and ran up the staircase to the second floor, noise be damned. A quick look through every bedroom, a study and closets got him nowhere. With no sign of Jolie or of Jesse Allen anywhere in the house, Devin's chest tightened.

Where would Jesse have taken Jolie? How could he have sneaked her out with a houseful of guests?

Devin returned to the staircase, taking the steps two at a time to the bottom. No one stopped to question him. Everyone else had left.

What was keeping Ash?

In Devin's mind, the clock was ticking for Jolie. If he didn't find her soon…

He didn't take that thought further. He'd find her. And when he did, he'd shake her until her teeth rattled for scaring the fool out of him. The only room he hadn't checked on the first floor was the kitchen.

He raced through. Dirty plates, pots and pans had been left piled in the sink. Why would Allen send the staff home before cleaning up? Unless he wanted to be alone with Jolie.

The thought chilled Devin to the core. He couldn't lose Jolie now. He loved her.

He came to a complete halt in the middle of the messy kitchen, his focus crystallizing as what he knew in his heart exploded through his senses. He loved Jolie Carson. Why he hadn't seen it sooner, he didn't know. As Natalie had said, Jolie had been under his nose for the past six years, quietly making his life better by the smile on her face, her laughter and her genuine concern for him and his family.

Had it taken making love to her and nearly losing her to bring him to his senses? What a fool he'd been.

And he'd be damned if he'd lose her now. He had to find her and tell her.

He tore through the kitchen door out into the night air. The five-car garage loomed in front of him. Jolie wasn't anywhere in the house. Her car was nowhere to be found outside. What were the chances it would be in Jesse Allen's garage? Slim.

Devin couldn't leave it to chance. He entered the garage, noting it hadn't been locked. Inside he came to a halt. Despite the limited lighting and his lack of a flashlight, he recognized the car in the first stall immediately. Jolie's pearly-white four-door Altima. She'd been so proud of that car when she'd bought it new off the lot. Her first, she'd said, having always purchased used cars to keep the costs down. She'd beamed so brightly at a board meeting, the board of directors had all commented.

Only one stall remained empty; the others had cars with cloth covers protecting their finish. Had Jesse taken Jolie somewhere in the missing car?

Devin almost groaned at the prospect. If Jesse had left the grounds with Jolie, they could be almost anywhere in or around the city of St. Louis. Devin wondered if Ash could get the police to look up the vehicles Jesse Allen owned and put out an APB on the one missing from the garage. He pulled his cell phone from his pocket to dial Ash but didn't have reception. He was considering going outside to get a signal when he spotted the door at the opposite end of the garage.

Before he called in the big guns, he had to check everywhere, even the office off the garage.

He entered expecting to find nothing. Too worried about Jolie to care if he got caught, Devin switched the light on. The office had little to offer in the way of space, but it had yet another door. Beside the door a bolt cutter leaned against the wall and the remains of a lock lay on the floor beside it. On the desk was a woman's purse, one he'd seen Jolie carry on occasion.

Devin's heart skipped several beats, then slammed into his rib cage, rushing blood through his system. Jolie had been here. Had she forced the lock and gotten caught? If so, was she inside the room, held by Jesse Allen? She could be in danger, hurt, maybe…

Devin gulped down the fear rising to choke off his air. He switched the light off, eased open the door with the latch and heard voices rising up from the darkness below.

Chapter Sixteen

"Why, Jesse?" Jolie asked, stalling for time while she worked through her options. "Why are you stalking the Kendalls and me? What did we ever do to you?"

"You of all people should know by now. The Kendalls are heartless, soulless murderers who don't care about anybody, just the almighty dollar."

"That's not true. The Kendalls care. They're involved in charities. They sponsor orphanages in both Tanzania and Uganda. They've donated millions to special-needs children in the United States. They do more than most large corporations with the money they earn."

"No." Jesse stepped forward, his eyes narrowing. "They play God with people's lives. They crush dreams and take away livelihoods without a thought as to the repercussions."

"What are you talking about?"

"It doesn't matter." Jesse moved closer.

"Obviously it does." Jolie had her back to the wall, but she lifted her chin, refusing to show the fear rising in her heart. Jesse said she'd never leave the wine cellar alive. If Jolie let that happen, she'd never have the chance to tell Devin how she really felt, never let him know that she loved him.

She'd kept that secret to herself for so long until the

other day when she'd told Natalie. Having told her friend had been a cathartic experience in itself, unleashing the possibilities.

If she survived Jesse's threat, what did she have to lose by telling Devin she loved him?

Her fingers tightened around the items in her hands. The penlight and the letter opener she'd taken from Jesse's office. So wrapped up in her discovery of Jesse's obsession, she'd almost forgotten she had them. She hid the letter opener in the folds of her black dress, waiting for her opportunity to escape.

"Who are you talking about? Whose dreams did the Kendalls crush?" Jolie asked. The longer Jesse talked, the more time she had to maneuver her way toward possible escape.

"Letty Morgan."

"The woman who quit from the mail room?"

"She's one."

"How did you know about her?"

His lip curled in a sneer. "I've had my eye on Kendall Communications."

"If you'd bothered to do your homework, you'd know she wasn't doing her job. She didn't come to work half the time and she was doing drugs. Devin gave her chances and an offer of professional counseling. The woman was wrapped up in drugs and her loser boyfriend kept supplying her. We couldn't keep her on. Even so, she quit before Devin could fire her."

"What about Juan Alvarez?"

Jolie's frown cleared as she remembered the photograph she'd seen in the desk upstairs. The one she had taken a picture of. "Was he your father?"

"He is still, what's left of him. Craig Kendall took everything my father had. His job, his home, the future of his children."

Jolie shook her head. "I can't believe Craig would do that. He's a kindhearted man."

"He did. My father worked as groundskeeper for Joseph and Marie Kendall. Everything would have been fine had they lived. But no—Craig Kendall had to go and murder them."

"Craig didn't kill them. The evidence you have against him is only circumstantial. It won't hold up in court. And isn't it a little bit funny how your prize witness isn't around to testify?" Jolie leaned forward. "Are you into manipulating the law to include disposing of witnesses after they've signed a confession?"

"Shut up." Jesse closed the distance between them in a single move, clutching her throat with one big hand. "I did what had to be done. Kendall deserves the chair for what he did to my father and me."

Jolie gasped for breath, forcing the words past her lips. "Is that what this is all about? You want revenge on the Kendalls for something they did to your father?"

"It's more than that."

Jolie stared into Jesse's eyes, the meaning of the letters, the picture of his family, the girl Jesse was with wearing matching sweatshirts coming together. "You blame the Kendalls for ruining *your* life. You loved her, didn't you?"

His grip tightened on her throat, lifting her off her feet.

Jolie held the letter opener, poised, ready to use when she had no other choice. That moment neared as inevitably as death. "Who was she? What was her name?" she asked, her voice straining against the hand pressing into her vocal cords.

"Emma." The one word broke from his mouth in a tight, strangled sob. His grip slackened enough that Jolie's feet touched ground, but not enough she could break free easily. "When my father lost his job, my world fell apart. I lost my scholarship to school and I lost...Emma."

"Did she know how much you loved her?" Jolie asked. She didn't want to stab the man. If she could convince him to let go of his hatred, to let her leave, she might make it out alive, without a struggle. Her heart bled for the man. To have loved and lost like he had hurt.

All too soon Jolie would be in the same situation. Once her engagement was over, her connection to the Kendalls would be forever severed. She'd go one way, Devin would go another. What would it be like to never again see the one you loved?

Jolie stared into Jesse's face and knew. The pain was reflected in the lines around the man's eyes and lips. "She must have been special."

"How would I know? I didn't get the chance to find out." Jesse's hand squeezed harder, digging into her neck. "I want them to hurt like I have. Like my father has. I want them to know the pain of losing someone they love. Unfortunately for you, that means Devin losing you."

Jolie snorted. "That's where you are wrong. Devin Kendall doesn't love me. Our engagement is a fake."

Jesse Allen's eyes widened, his face growing red beneath the swarthy tan. "You're lying."

"No, I'm not. We only staged the engagement to take focus off the gossips and keep it on the murder investigation." She smiled, despite the pain he inflicted against her throat. "Killing me will not faze the Kendalls in any way." Sadly, every word Jolie spoke was true. Natalie had said Devin loved her. Jolie knew better. Devin loved his family to the exclusion of all others.

Jesse roared, his hand pushing her up the wall. "Liar!"

Jolie dropped the penlight and clawed at the hand holding her throat. She couldn't breathe and panic crept in. Gray fog tainted the edges of her vision. It was now or never. She raised her hand, ready to thrust.

DEVIN TOOK THE STEPS two at a time, the sound of voices growing louder. One of them he recognized as Jolie's. Thank heavens. He'd found her.

As he passed row after row of wine racks, he heard Jesse Allen shout, "Liar!"

At that moment, Devin cleared the last rack, rounding the corner to discover a small work area at the back of the cellar.

Allen, dressed in a tailored black suit, stood with his back to Devin, holding Jolie in front of him.

A foot kicked out and the high heel dangling from it fell to the ground.

Devin rushed forward, shouting, "Let her go!"

Jesse Allen spun, whipping Jolie around into the crook of his arm. "One more step and I snap her neck."

Devin ground to a halt, panic seizing the air from his lungs. "Let her go, Jesse. She's done nothing to you."

"She was trespassing. Snooping through my belongings."

"She's no threat to you. Let her go."

"What do you know about threats? I'll show you threat." Jesse tightened his hold on Jolie's neck. "Your lover can't breathe. She's getting weaker. She'll die in minutes. How's that for a threat?"

"Let her go or…" Devin searched the area for something, anything he could use as a weapon.

"Or what? You'll murder me?" He laughed. "Shall we chalk up another murder to the Kendall family? You all seem so good at it."

"Look, Jesse, I know about your father. I know you

blame the Kendalls for his losing your family home. I know you had to drop out of college to help him. But you can't destroy what you've worked so hard to build. You can't let the past determine your future. Killing Jolie proves nothing. It will only make you lose everything. Even worse than what happened to your father. Not only will you lose your home, you'll lose your freedom, maybe even your life."

Jesse laughed, his movement jerking Jolie around. Her pale skin had gone a deathly gray, but her eyes were open, her lips moving, no sound coming out.

Devin stepped forward. He had to get to Jolie.

"Don't." Jesse kept Jolie in front of him, his arm tight around her throat, his other hand clamping down on her forehead. "All it takes is a quick twist and her neck snaps."

"Let her go. You can do whatever you want with me, just let her go."

"I have you now, don't I?" Jesse laughed again. "Now you'll know how it feels to lose the one you love. Just like I did."

"No, please." Devin reached out. "Please, don't kill her. You're right. I love her. I'd do anything for her. Just don't kill her."

Jolie's eyes widened, tears spilling from them. Her hand moved at her side.

Before Devin realized what she held, her wrist came up and jammed downward, hitting against Allen's leg.

Jesse screamed, his arm loosening around Jolie's throat. He shoved Jolie away from him and doubled over, clutching at the sharp metal object protruding from his thigh.

Jolie fell forward, rolled to the side and lay as still as death.

Jesse yanked what looked like a knife from his leg, his lips pulled back in a snarl, his hand fisting around the weapon, his gaze locking in on Jolie's inert form. He roared and lunged for Jolie.

Devin plowed into him, knocking him off his feet and into the desk behind him.

Jesse bellowed like an enraged bull, twisted and rolled off the desk, grabbing Devin and taking him down with him.

Devin dodged the thrust of the dagger and grabbed for Jesse's wrist as they both hit the floor hard.

Devin took the brunt of the fall, Jesse's body slamming him into the hard concrete. The breath knocked from him, Devin maintained his grip on the wrist holding the long, thin blade.

The two struggled for control, Jesse with the advantage of being on top.

Then a flash of red hair blurred Devin's vision as Jolie flung herself onto Jesse's back, clawing, kicking and biting.

If Devin wasn't in such a precarious position holding on to a deadly weapon, he'd have laughed out loud at the comical picture of Jolie jumping the district attorney.

Yet, there was nothing funny about the crazed look in Jesse's eyes, nor the strength of his arm baring down on the weapon.

"You and your family will pay for what you did to me and mine."

"You're insane, Jesse," Devin said through gritted teeth. His arms shook with the strain of holding Jesse off.

Jolie appeared above them holding a full bottle of wine.

Devin saw the bottle crash down a second before it hit Jesse in the head. The glass shattered, the liquid drenching Jesse's head and splashing down into Devin's eyes.

Jesse slumped forward, his full weight crushing the air out of Devin's lungs.

Devin shoved and scooted his way across the wet floor until he could sit up, brushing sticky red liquid from his face. "Good thinking."

Jolie held out her hand to him.

Devin grasped it, but before he could pull himself up, Jolie shoved him to the side.

Jesse lunged upward, the knife meant for Devin's back plunging into Jolie's chest.

Devin elbowed Jesse in the face. The sound of snapping cartilage split the air and Jesse fell backward, blood pouring from his nose.

Devin leaped to his feet, ready to finish Jesse off.

A hand on his shoulder stopped him. "I'll take it from here." Ash pushed Devin to the side. "You call for an ambulance. Jolie needs help."

Devin spun to where Jolie had dropped to her knees, her hands going to the blade protruding from her chest. Her eyes were round and glazed, her face so pale she looked like death.

Devin dropped down beside her and caught her wrists to keep her from pulling the blade from her chest. "Don't. Taking it out may cause more damage than leaving it for the doctors to remove." He didn't know how he managed to keep his voice calm, but he did.

Jolie was going into shock. Losing it now would do no good for either of them. She had to remain extremely still or suffer more internal damage.

He pulled his phone from his pocket, thankful he had a small amount of reception.

"I need an ambulance." He rattled off the address to the dispatcher. "Please, hurry." Despite his resolution to remain strong, Devin's words shook. He turned to Jolie, whose gaze had moved from the blade protruding from her chest to him.

"Devin?" Her voice came out in a whisper.

"Yeah, baby." He slipped an arm around her and held on, feeling so helpless he wanted to die. He stroked the hair from her face.

"The proposal we were working on for the Jenkins buyout is on my desk."

Devin laughed, the sound more of a sob than anything. "Forget about the proposal. It's the last thing I want to think about right now."

"But you'll need it for the board meeting tomorrow."

"Board meeting be damned." He faced her, holding her arms carefully so as not to jar her body. His own chest ached with the need to take away her pain. "Shouldn't you be resting or something?"

"No," she said, her voice tight, her gaze capturing his. A single tear slipped from the corner of her eye. "I'm afraid if I…"

He pressed a finger to her lips. "Don't say it. Don't even think it. It's just a flesh wound." His voice tripped over the words, a knot the size of Illinois blocked his throat. "You're going to be fine. Besides, Natalie and my aunt would have my hide if they can't go wedding dress shopping with you."

"You and I know this engagement was a fake." Jolie lifted a hand to Devin's face, a smile tipping the corners of her lips. "But just in case I don't get to say it, I love you." Her body tensed and her shoulders hunched. Jolie's eyes squeezed closed, her pale face blanching white.

"Jolie, don't go dropping bombs on me like that and then skipping out."

"Didn't I tell you I quit?" The words came out in a breathy whisper as her body leaned into his.

Ash jerked Jesse Allen to his feet. "I'm taking him up top to meet with my backups and to direct the emergency personnel down here. I have a blanket in my car, but not much else in the way of first-responder equipment. Will you two be all right?"

"Nothing a good stiff drink won't cure." Jolie laughed, the slight movement causing her to cringe. "Remind me not to laugh."

Devin cringed with her. "Remind me not to let you out of my sight ever again."

"Can't make any promises." She leaned on his shoulder. "I've always wanted to do this."

"What, get stabbed in the chest?"

"Be held in your arms."

"Count on a lot more of that when we have you all patched up."

"Don't tease me, Devin. I won't be your own personal pity date."

"Pity date? Is that what you think?" He wanted to shake her, but settled for shaking his own head. "It took me six years to realize what I should have discovered the first day you walked into my office."

"That you shouldn't have hired me?"

"No, that I love you."

A tear slid down her cheek. "I told you I didn't want your pity."

"You aren't getting it. Well, maybe for a week or two until you recover, but after that. All bets off."

"And our engagement will be at an end."

Before Devin could refute her statement, footsteps thundered down the steps as emergency medical technicians filled the wine cellar.

They laid Jolie out on a stretcher, carefully stabilizing the blade in her chest to avoid movement and further internal damage.

Devin stood out of the way, his heart now in the hands

of the men and women who would see Jolie to the trauma unit at St. Louis University Hospital.

He followed them up the stairs and out of the garage where emergency vehicles choked the driveway and a helicopter stood waiting in the nearby cul-de-sac.

As they loaded Jolie into the helicopter, Ash joined him, his hand clamping down on Devin's shoulder. "Let's go. I have a blue-light special that'll get us to the hospital almost as fast as the helicopter."

Devin nodded and turned away as the rotors on the helicopter spun to life.

"I have to get there. Jolie needs me." Devin walked fast, his footsteps eating the distance to Ash's car.

"That's a first." Ash broke into a jog to keep up with Devin. "You're the one that always needed her."

"And I still do, more than I need to breathe."

Chapter Seventeen

A bright light shone down on Jolie as her eyes blinked open. Had she died? Was that the light she was supposed to move toward? "Am I dead?" she said out loud, her voice no more than a hoarse whisper.

The twitter of laughter warmed her insides, bringing focus from the overhead light fixture to the woman sitting beside her bed.

Natalie patted her hand. "Honey, you're not going anywhere. The Kendalls are in agreement, you're a part of this family and we want you to stick around for a long time."

"Hi, Natalie." Jolie forced a smile to her cracked lips.

"Here, I'll bet you're thirsty. You've been out for twelve hours since the surgery."

Jolie's head lifted from the pillow as she tried to get a look at her chest.

"Don't worry, the surgeon removed the blade. Good Lord, I saw it. Looked like a letter opener."

A sharp pain stabbed across her chest and Jolie fell back against the pillow. "It was."

"You're supposed to let us help if you want to sit up. No strain on your chest for a few days. But after that, you're expected to recover fully. You're a lucky girl."

"How is getting stabbed in the chest lucky?"

"It missed all the important stuff, like the heart…you know, vital organs. It did nick one of your lungs, but the hole was small enough the doctor said it would close on its own. And because you didn't yank the blade out, you didn't get all that nasty air between your lung tissue and chest cavity. That's what had them worried. All they had to do was remove, patch and *voilà!*"

"I don't feel so *voilà*." Jolie shut her eyes to the light above. "How's Devin?"

"A few bumps and bruises, but business as usual, running around shouting orders to anyone who'll listen." Natalie smiled. "He's got the nurses eating out of his hand and the doctors jumping when he says jump."

"Oh, dear."

"Not to worry, the doctor said he'll release you as soon as you prove you can get out of bed on your own."

Jolie opened her eyes. "That's a relief."

"A lot has been happening since you've been asleep."

The door opened and a head poked inside. "Hello. Anyone awake?" Craig Kendall's eyes lit up when he saw Jolie's eyes open. "Oh, good, you're finally awake."

Jolie smiled up at the man she admired and had grown to love almost like a father. "Craig. How did you…did Jesse confess…thank goodness…" She tried to sit up again, but Natalie's hand on her shoulder kept her flat.

"I told you a lot has happened." Natalie turned to her uncle. "Where's Ash?"

"Right behind me." Craig looked over his shoulder.

"I'm right here." Ash pushed the door wide and entered, a smile on his face and a bouquet of brightly colored gerbera daisies in his hands. "Is our hero awake and up to visitors?"

"I'm awake, but I don't know about visitors. I'm sure I'm a wreck." She pressed a hand to her hair, the tangles more than she cared to tackle at the moment. "What you see is what you get."

"To be expected after what you went through. Rachel sent these up. She said she'd have come up but figured the nurses would chase us all out if we had too many people in the room at once." His eyes widened as he looked around. "Holy cow, did the flower shop explode in here?"

Natalie took the vase from her brother and placed it on the wide windowsill with at least a dozen other bouquets.

"Wow," Jolie said, tears rushing to fill her eyes. "I just noticed those."

"A lot of people were worried about you. There have been so many calls and flowers from all the people whose lives you've touched at Kendall Communications. Face it, girl—" Natalie leaned over and gave her a gentle hug "—you're loved." She straightened and wiped a tear from her eye.

"Yup, and for what you did for all of us…let me just say thanks," Craig added.

Jolie shook her head. "But I didn't do anything."

"Girl, you've been out for a while." Natalie nodded at Ash. "Tell her."

"Maybe I should let Devin."

Jolie laughed, pain shooting through her chest. "Please, don't make me laugh, just tell me."

"I had my boys at the precinct conduct a more in-depth, nationwide background check on Gene Williams, the conveniently dead confessor. Seems he couldn't have been the murderer that killed our parents," Ash said.

"Why?" Jolie asked.

"He wasn't even in St. Louis at the time of the murders." Ash grinned. "They managed to find a buddy of his who claimed he was in an L.A. hospital for stab wounds from a gang fight. They were able to track down the hospital and records of his visit to the emergency room the night of our parents' deaths."

"As soon as the police discovered that, they informed the judge, who demanded my immediate release," Craig finished.

"I'm so glad." Jolie smiled at the older man. "I hated the thought of you in that jail."

Craig laughed. "You and me both. It was an...interesting experience. One I hope never to repeat."

"What happened to Jesse Allen?" Jolie asked.

"When he found out his prime witness's story didn't check out, he realized he'd been caught falsifying a confession. He went ballistic, shouting profanities about the Kendalls. Before his own lawyer could arrive, he'd confessed to a lot of things that will land him in jail for a very long time."

Jolie frowned. "How'd he get Gene to confess to murder in the first place?"

"He told the guy he'd post his bond and give him enough money to skip the country. Only Allen never planned on letting Williams skip town."

"Allen was charged with the murder of Gene Williams and your attempted murder." Natalie brushed the hair off Jolie's forehead. "By the way, thanks for taking the fall for my big brother. I'll get to tease him about that for the rest of his life." She leaned over and kissed Jolie's forehead. "No, really, you saved his life. Thanks."

Jolie's face heated. Pushing Devin out of the way hadn't been an act of self-sacrifice, it had been purely selfish. She wanted him alive so that she could continue to love him, even if it was from a distance. She swallowed her confession, not quite ready to admit to a roomful of Kendalls that she was a complete sap and still head over heels in love with Devin.

"What about the real murderer?" Jolie asked, diverting attention away from herself.

Ash shook his head, his smile fading. "The case is still under investigation. We haven't turned up any more clues, but they're working it."

Jolie sighed. "At least Craig isn't the prime suspect." She closed her eyes, sending up a silent prayer for the murderer to be found before someone else got hurt.

"Come on, she's tired," Craig said.

Jolie's eyes opened. "I'm fine, really."

"You need your rest. We just wanted to stop in and let you know how we felt." Ash closed the distance between them and bent over to press a kiss to her forehead, as Natalie had done earlier. "You're part of the family now, and we don't want to lose you anytime soon."

Craig repeated the gesture. "Angela has been gathering bride magazines. Soon as you're up to it, she's got shopping plans for you. Take care." He smiled and left the room.

Natalie stood beside her, rocking back on her heels. "I have to go now, too. I have a cup of coffee with my name on it getting cold in the waiting room."

Jolie caught Natalie's hand before she could leave. "Thanks for being here."

"It was nothing. I've only been here for a little more than ten minutes. Devin wouldn't let any of us near you until I told him he'd scare you into a seizure the way he looked."

"Yeah, he looked like crap." Ash rested his hands on Natalie's shoulders. "He refused to leave the hospital for even a second. The doctors let him use the shower in the doctors' lounge to clean up, I think out of self-preservation. He was starting to smell."

Natalie glanced at her watch. "He should be back any

minute." Natalie looked up and smiled as the door swung open. "Speak of the devil."

Devin Kendall filled the doorway, his brown hair gleaming wet and a full day's beard darkening his jaw. He looked so beautiful Jolie thought maybe she had died and gone to heaven after all. He stood holding the door for Natalie, his gaze on Jolie, his blue eyes so intense Jolie squirmed.

Her hand rose to her hair, lying in a tangled mass against the pillow. "My hair's—"

"Beautiful."

"Liar."

"That's our cue," Ash said, turning Natalie toward the door. "Come on, Nat."

Natalie chuckled. "Sure I can't stay?"

"Leave." Devin jerked his head toward the door.

Ash grabbed his sister's hand and dragged her through and the door swung closed behind her.

"Spoilsport." Natalie's muffled voice carried through the closed door.

Devin crossed the room and stood beside Jolie's bed, gathering her hand in his, careful not to bump the IV needle. "Hey."

"Hey." Jolie almost laughed at the stilted greeting. Her empty stomach knotted. Memories of her near-death confession filled her mind and burned her cheeks with embarrassment. How much would he remember? Would he hold it against her? Would he pity her for loving him? "I'd appreciate it if you'd just forget anything stupid I might have said when I thought I was dying."

"You said something stupid?" His eyes widened, and he was the picture of innocence. He pulled the chair up close to her and sat, still holding her hand. "Can't recall. Perhaps you could remind me."

Tears filled her eyes again for the second time in as many minutes. What was wrong with her? She never cried. She blinked, trying to hold them back, but one fell, then another.

Devin reached out and captured one tear with his finger. "Hey, what's this?"

"Nothing." She sniffed. "Must be dust in my eyes."

"Jolie, I have something I need to tell you." He stared down at her fingers for a long time.

Jolie's heart bounced to the pit of her stomach and back up to lodge somewhere in her throat. She couldn't say anything even had she found words. He was trying to let her down easy. She cleared her throat, the pain it caused in her chest helping to fortify her resolve. "Don't. I know what you're going to say."

He looked up, a frown drawing his brows together. "You do?"

"Yes. I don't want you to feel at all obligated to say anything you'll regret out of some misguided gratitude or sense of duty."

Devin's lips twitched. "Is that what I was going to say?"

Jolie pulled her hand from his. "Let me finish."

He nodded, crossing his arms over his chest. "Please, go on. It's amazing how I don't even have to open my mouth and you put words right into it."

"Don't tease. This is hard enough without you making jokes."

He drew a line over his lips and sealed them, light sparkling in his eyes.

Had Jolie been up to it, she'd have launched a pillow at him. "Seriously, Devin. This is not a joke to me."

"I didn't say it was."

"I told you I loved you because I thought I was dying." There, she'd said it.

"And now that you're not dying, you're going to retract your statement?"

"No, that's not it. Don't confuse me, my head's still fuzzy." She pressed a hand to her temple. "You and I are from different worlds. What we had between us that night in your apartment was, well…"

"Beautiful, incredible, amazing."

"Well, yes. But that's not the point."

He leaned forward, all humor wiped from his expression. "Then what is?"

"We don't have to continue with the fake engagement. It's not fair to your family or to you."

"What if I don't want to end it? What if I want it to be real?"

Jolie's heart skipped several beats and she attempted to sit up, ignoring the pain shooting through her. "Don't make me sit up. It hurts too much."

"Then lie down and let me talk for a change. Sheesh, woman, you boss me around in the office, you boss me around in the hospital. Is this any indication of how you'll boss me around in our marriage?" He smiled down at her, softening his teasing words.

"That's just it, we don't have to fake an engagement anymore."

"You're absolutely right." He stood, pushing back the chair.

Jolie gulped. "I'm right?"

"The *fake* engagement is officially off." Devin sucked in a deep breath, let it out, then dropped to one knee beside her bed. His head was a little lower than hers as he held her hand. "Let's make it real."

Jolie's head twisted to the side and she stared into his eyes. "What did you say?"

"Jolie Carson, you're my hero, my salvation and the

only woman I would ever consider spending the rest of my life with. Will you marry me?"

"Didn't you listen to anything I said? We're not from the same worlds. I don't belong in yours."

"And what world would that be? We live on the same planet." He smiled, his free hand brushing the hair back off Jolie's forehead. "As far as I'm concerned, the only world I want to live in is one with you in it."

"What about your family?"

"You're a part of it."

"But I'm just a secretary...." Her argument grew weaker. She wanted him so much and had loved him for so long.

"Executive assistant and soon to be promoted to partner." He stood and gazed down at her. "I love you, Jolie, and want you to be my wife. Please just say yes."

Jolie stared up into his eyes. "But—"

"Using the words of a very wise woman, stop thinking of reasons you can't and start thinking of reasons you can." He leaned close, his lips hovering over hers. "Start with the answer to the most important question. Do you love me?"

With his lips only a breath away from hers, she couldn't think to lie. "Yes."

"Then there's only one other question you need to answer. Will you marry me?" He brushed her lips gently, then backed up enough to look into her eyes.

She could fall into those blue eyes. She loved this man more than she loved life. How could she even consider living without him? And why should she? He was asking her to marry him, for heaven's sake. Jolie reached up with her free hand, encircling Devin's neck, bringing his lips back to hers. "Yes."

He kissed her, then laughed out loud. "You won't regret it, Jolie. I promise to make you happy."

She smiled up at him through tear-filled eyes. "You already have."

* * * * *

On impulse, he unfolded himself from the bar stool. "Need a hand?"

"Thank you! I…" She lifted her gaze from the floor to his jeans and then raised her eyes. When she identified him her hazel eyes turned from grateful to unfriendly and cold, as if he'd somehow thrown the broken glasses at her head.

He also thought he saw a glimmer of panic in those interesting depths, which instantly stirred his curiosity like cream swirling through coffee.

"I've got it, Officer. Thank you." Her voice was several degrees colder than the whirl of sleet outside the windows.

Despite her protests, he knelt down beside her and began to pick up shards of broken glass. "No problem. Those trays can be slippery."

This close, he picked up the scent of her, something fresh and flowery that made him think of a mountain meadow on a July afternoon. She had a soft, lush mouth and for one brief, insane moment, he wanted to push aside that stray lock of hair slipping from her ponytail and taste her. Apparently he needed to spend a lot less time working and a great deal *more* time recreating with the opposite sex if he could have sudden random fantasies about a woman he wasn't even inclined to like, pretty or not.

"I'm Trace Bowman. You must be new in town."

She didn't answer immediately and he could almost see the wheels turning in her head. Why the hesitancy? And why that little hint of unease he could see clouding the edge of her gaze? His presence was obviously making her uncomfortable and Trace couldn't help wondering why.

"Yes. We've been here a few weeks."

"Well, I'm just up the road about four lots, in the white house with the cedar shake roof, if you or your daughter need anything." He smiled at her as he picked up the last shard of glass and set it on her tray.

Definitely a story there, he thought as she hurried away. He just might need to dig a little into her background to find out why someone with fine clothes and nice jewelry, and who so obviously didn't have experience as a waitress, would be here slinging hash at The Gulch. Was she running away from someone? A bad marriage?

So…Rebecca Parsons. Not Becky. An intriguing woman. It had been a long time since one of those had crossed his path here in Pine Gulch.

Trace won't rest until he finds out Rebecca's secret, but will he still have that same attraction to her once he does? Find out in CHRISTMAS IN COLD CREEK. Available November 2011 from Harlequin® Special Edition®.

Harlequin®

ROMANTIC
SUSPENSE

CARLA CASSIDY

Cowboy's Triplet Trouble

Jake Johnson, the eldest of his triplet brothers, is stunned
when Grace Sinclair turns up on his family's ranch declaring
Jake's younger and irresponsible brother as the father of her
triplets. When Grace's life is threatened, Jake finds himself
fighting a powerful attraction and a need to protect. But as
the threats hit closer to home, Jake begins to wonder
if someone on the ranch is out to kill Grace....

A brand-new Top Secret Deliveries story!

TOP SECRET
DELIVERIES

Available in November wherever books are sold!

HRS27751